THE
SHARON SLAUGHTER
STORY

BY BLACK MAMBA

THE
SHARON SLAUGHTER STORY

1976

On the 18th of August 1976, at the Misericordia Hospital, located in the depths of Black Philadelphia, a black female demon was born. She was born addicted to cocaine and heroin and ironically her last name would be Malo. The Malo family was a plethora of drug addicts, prostitutes, murderers and any other criminally insane category one could imagine. Her mother Vera was the utmost definition of a drug-addicted super criminal. Vera's cocaine and heroin addiction drove her to engage in any crime that fit the bill to feed her ever-growing narcotic habit. This habit became so dominant that it outgrew Vera's mind and controlled her until it became the very essence of her existence. She lived, dreamed, and utterly believed in narcotics in their entirety. Her body was so polluted with narcotics that this birth, her only one, was deemed impossible. The birth of this infant was a miracle in a demented, hellspawn miraculous way. For she was born out of a narcotic laden, seemingly barren womb and conceived with an unknown father. It was a quasi-immaculate conception. So, on this humid day with the sun shining in the constellation Leo, she was born without wailing a single sound. As was customary the doctor patted the infant on her back to hear the cry a usual newborn would produce to indicate that all was well. However, after three attempts the infant merely giggled. Bizarre as it seemed, the doctor had indeed viewed this scene before.

"All of her vitals are good but let me tell you from my experience a baby that laughs when they are first born is going to be one mean mother jumper! I think my mother-in-law was born laughing up a storm," laughed the doctor while taking off his rubber gloves.

Vera looked at the infant with malice in her heart.

'This motherfucking little Cabbage Patch Kids looking bitch done took six God damn long ass hours to get here and she got the fucking nerve to laugh! On everything I love, I got a good mind to shove this motherfucker back up my ass and go score me some slow and blow! Sho'nuff!' Vera thought to herself. When the attending nurse asked Vera if she wanted to hold the baby she declined to the nurse's dismay.

"BITCH you hold her! I gots to piss!" roared Vera in aggression. The Nurse did so for over an hour before she realized that Vera had not only left but she'd also taken an almost full bag of medical morphine with her. Hours later when Vera returned high and unconcerned, she was encountered by a senior nurse who was not the least bit intimidated by her.

"Don't be so loud, you blasphemous drug addict! Now I knew when your sack of no-good ass bones came in here you was going to be trouble! I had a daughter just like your trifling ass! So when the nurse assistant called me up here and told me you left, shit, I started to call Child Services. But when I came up here and laid eyes on this precious child, I just couldn't. If you would not have come back I would have gladly took this baby home and lost my job so she could have a chance at life! Now you going to sit your narrow ass down and feed her this formula when she wakes up and let the doctors stitch your simple ass up! You ain't even name the child! You ran out of here as soon as she came out! Pussy wide open like a deli and you out there turning tricks like double dutch! Got the nerve to be high! Sit your ass down and tend to this child while I go get the doctor. And you better tell me this child's name so I can mark it down. Now what is it?"

Vera stared at the plump older black woman with a heap of scorn but a slight touch of apathy.

Deep down inside she knew the woman was right, yet the narcotics controlled her mind.

"Sharon! Sharon is her name! Now take your raggedy old fat ass somewhere and give me my child", she puffed in half a nod as she glanced at the old woman's name tag which read "Sharon".

The old nurse glared at Vera with blazing eyes full of loving contempt before jotting down her name and number on a small piece of paper.

"Here is my number in case you want to change your life you little heifer! Now lay down and take them God awful smelling clothes off so the doctor can tend to your no-good ass," announced the old nurse as she placed the small piece of paper on a nearby table and exited the room.

Vera glided over to the small piece of paper and looked at it and then she looked at her sleeping infant. She repeated this routine for several seconds while the nod caused her to lay on the bed until the doctor came. *'Old fat bitch smell like mothballs and fuckin Newports,'* she thought to herself as the effects of heroin caused her to fade into the land of nod.

The loud, continuous ring of the doorbell snapped a middle-aged Caucasian woman out of her afternoon nap and brought her to full attention. Glancing at herself in a mirror before answering the door she imagined it was her twenty-year-old boyfriend whom she was having an affair with in secret unbeknownst to her husband. That ridiculous fantasy was cut short as she viewed the massive amount of makeup on her wrinkled face.

'Who would want my huge prehistoric ass?' she pondered to herself.

The constant ringing of the doorbell rushed got her to leave the mirror and rush to the front of the house. Opening the door, she was astonished at what she saw- a newborn baby neatly tucked in a colorful Easter basket. Shocked, she made an attempt to lay hold to the child but was instantly apprehended at gunpoint.

"Bitch back up in the house 'fore I blow your head clean smooth off! Bitch move," ordered the assailant behind the veil of a grey bandana.

The middle-aged woman was positive that the perpetrator was female despite the effort to disguise. The masked gunmen pushed the middle-aged woman inside the house with enough force to send her crashing to the floor. The middle-aged woman was so frightened she dared not to make a sound. A second assailant then entered the home and closed the front door, leaving the newborn on the porch. With the addition of a second assailant the victim grew even more terrified. "Please! Please wait! My purse is on the kitchen counter! I have a jewelry case in my bedroom take it! Just please don't hurt me", begged the woman as she sat up on the living room floor. The female robber looked at the obviously male robber with a look of frustration as the male robber stood aloof, seemingly confused while scratching his neck with irritation.

"Char-lee! Char fuckin lee! If your simple ass don't go get that and come on! I swear before Christ Imma cap your goofy ass! Go get that," barked the female robber. The male robber scratched his head in confusion.

"Umm arghh, yeah umm what am I supposed to get Vera?"

At the mention of her name, the masked Vera began to physically assault the masked male robber. The victim squinted her eyes as she watched the comedy ridden criminal episode in which she was, for the minute, a victim. Slowly as the robbing duo scuffled, she inched her way to a nearby phone. Suddenly, Vera, now unmasked, grabbed the phone the victim intended to reach and savagely beat her with it until she stopped moving. "Charl-ee! Now stand here and watch this here peckerwood while I get all the shit! You silly dumb muthafucka!"

Charlee merely shrugged his shoulders and locked his eyes on the victim without moving a step.

Vera swooped through the house, located the items and vanished out the front door. Seconds later she reappeared and hit Charlee upside his head with a vicious haymaker.

"I swear to God! Charlee if you don't bring your stupid ass! Come on!"

"Vera you just ah…you just… you just told me to watch the ah…the ah…ah peckerwood! You ah…ah…tell me to go nowhere! I'm ah I'm plum sick of ah ah… you hitting me! Now…ah ah…"

"Charlee go the fuck to the car! Stuttering muthafucka," barked Vera as she assaulted Charlee all the way out the front door. She even managed to push him down the front steps, dragging him along while carrying not just the stolen items, but also the newborn to the getaway car. There, fortunately for Charlee, he knew his role was to just drive off.

Vera and Charlee were professional squatters. Charlee would seek out an appropriate abandoned home, clean and clear it out, while he illegally wired electricity to the location. He was a skilled handyman by trade, drug addict by Vera's hand. Charlee hailed from Starkville, North Carolina. He came to Philadelphia in search of job opportunities, instead he met Vera prostituting on North Broad Street and he had been a derelict drug addict ever since. As low aptitude as he was, Vera loved Charlee. Not in the spirit of love itself but for the simple fact that he was dumbstruck in love with her to the point of obsession and she could control him to her sick delight. He worshipped the very ground Vera got high on. This might appear strange to a regular person, but there was a hidden dynamic to their relationship. Vera was rather attractive in appearance despite her outlandish living habits and massive drug addiction. She was still a sight for sore eyes. She was radiant in a ghetto way with hair that was long and of "Native Indian" stock while her skin was of a light brown hue. In her few drug-free crusader tangents, she cleaned up very well. This made her prostitution career flourish. Vera even shot narcotics in between her fingers and toes to avoid leaving visible track marks on her skin. Charlee on the other hand was short, stocky and rather difficult to look at for a long period of time. This also played into Vera's manipulation of his mind. Constantly, she reminded him of the fact that he had neither the looks nor the wherewithal to attract a woman of Vera's likeness. To make matters even worse, Charlee had an even lower self-esteem due to his excruciating stuttering. Add all of this together in a pot of crime and addiction and you have an atmosphere fit to raise the likes of Sharon

1986

"Char-lee Char-lee! Muthafucka I needs some light! How the fuck am I pose to get ready for the stroll and ain't no fucking light! Hurry up and hook that shit up you retarded muthafucka," spat Vera as Charlee fumbled about in the back alley nearby. Sharon sat close to Vera in an effort to watch her get dressed. She loved to watch her mother get ready to go out on "dates" as Vera called them. Before Vera could yell at Charlee again, the recently vacant house became illuminated with illegal light. Sharon smiled as she looked at her attractive mother dressed in a prostitute's finest: high heel boots, ripped stockings, short mini skirt and a face painted with heavy makeup. Vera cut her eyes at the smiling Sharon before she commented.

"What you smiling at you little stinking heifer! You always watching me get dressed! You ain't gonna be shit but a streetwalker! Watch!"

Vera and Sharon shared a twisted laugh. Sharon loved when her mother cursed, it excited her. As Vera found her purse and examined its contents, a special item caught her attention. Slowly, she unraveled the small piece of paper. It was the same piece of paper the senior nurse had given her the day Sharon was born. Often, in the midst of her lewd trappings, she would stare at the piece of paper and wonder how her life would be different if only, she could dial the number.

"Ah ah ah ah...Vera be be ah ah ah...careful honey...ah ah...give me ah ah...give me a kiss...ah ah love..."

Vera slapped Charlee across his face and kicked him in his scrotum sack as she snapped out of her redemption daze.

"Love you too babe," she said as she kissed Sharon on the forehead and sashayed out of the residence. She had a short walk from Pike Street to her stroll on Broad Street.

Charlee lay in pain on the floor. Only seconds before, Sharon had kicked and slapped him in a crude imitation of Vera. Sharon enjoyed inflicting pain on Charlee, it was her playtime of sorts. But what Sharon enjoyed more was her time alone with Charlee in which he told her of the many war stories from his father's experiences in the Korean War and his own experiences in the Vietnam War.

Sharon loved to hear stories about death and debauchery. Charlee didn't understand why, but he told her every gruesome experience he knew or heard of. It was how they bonded. Silently, Charlee wished Sharon was his actual child for he had none and Sharon looked at him as a father figure. Also, Charlee was infatuated with Sharon due to her being a spitting image of Vera. So on this hot summer night like any other night, Charlee would tell Sharon the most horrific stories from war he could recall as he cleaned the abandoned house and made it livable.

"Okay Charlee tell me about the really cool land mines!"

"Sh ah ah…shit Sharon! O…ah ah…o…ok!" He said, as he slowly got himself up off the ground before continuing.

"Viet-nam had all kinds of ah ah…landmines. Wait ah ah ah…one ah ah ah…minute." Charlee dusted himself off and picked up a broom.

"My friend good friend Darryl got blew up in front of me in Nam."

Sharon noticed that when Charlee spoke about extreme macabre vile memories from his past, he stuttered not.

"Yeah, I looked him right in the eye before pieces of his body flew into my face. I even tasted his flesh," he said in a low Southern drawl. Before he could continue, a single tear escaped his eye. He turned his body so Sharon would not see him cry, so she would not see the pain and hurt in his eyes. Little did he know not only could she sense the pain, but she loved to see the hurt in him. She actually loved to see the hurt and pain in anyone and anything. At the exact moment Charlee confided in her about his friend getting blown away by a landmine, Sharon wanted to blow Charlee up and taste his flesh, but she decided in her mind that an animal would do for now.

"Ah ah ah…ye ah ah…yeah his flesh tasted like real salty and hot…"

"Like steak Charlee? Cause I like hot steak! Boy it's good!"

Charlee turned around and found Sharon wide eyed and very attentive.

'Lord have mercy this child plum crazy,' he thought to himself before he commenced to cleaning again.

"Not so much so. More like ah ah…rabbit."

Sharon yelped and cheered so suddenly that it caused Charlee to spin around. She was cheering because in her young mind, blowing up a rabbit and tasting it was more plausible than blowing up and tasting Charlee. Charlee continued to confide in Sharon. An important detail that stuck out was that after Charlee watched his childhood friend explode in front of him due to a landmine, it took him weeks to speak out loud. When he finally did speak, it was with a terrible stutter. That was when he first started stuttering. Since then, he stuttered steadily, except for when he recalled eyewitness gruesome accounts or when he was high or intoxicated. The latter state brought a violent side out of Charlee, thus leading Vera to ban him from having access to alcohol.

Charlee rambled on and on about tales of bloody massacres and pernicious behavior while he was egged on with occasional questions and cheers from Sharon. But, in one instance as he was cleaning the kitchen, he heard no applause from Sharon and looked back to find her missing. Alarmed, Charlee began to call out and search for her. He checked every room and found no trace of her. Finally, he decided to go down into the basement.

Flipping on the basement light switch, he was surprised it did not produce any light. He swore by oath, he had, only moments ago, fixed the problem.

"Sh sh sh ah ah…Sharon! Ba ba ah ah…baby come on ah ah ah…from down there! I I I ah ah ah…I haven't cle cle cle…cleaned down there ye ye ye…yet!" Hearing no response, Charlee decided to check the basement. He reasoned Sharon had to be down there. Added to the fact, he knew she liked to play hide and seek. Upon taking his first step, he tripped over a tightly wound jump rope and crashed down the stairs onto the floor. On his back in pitch darkness, he was not only in pain, Charlee was terrified. Before he could let out a scream, Sharon flashed a flashlight upon her face right next to Charlee.

"Tripwire Charlee! Arggh, she yelled as she stabbed him with the screwdriver repeatedly. Charlee yelled out in painstaking agony and horror as Sharon roared in delight. He ran blindly in the dark and only managed to injure himself more by running into a pillar face-first. Sharon ran up the stairs, closing and locking the basement door behind her.

"Charlee you told me in Nam, Charlie was the enemy! You said it was spelled different but I'm not dumb! I'm ten! I'm not gonna let you out until you tell me what the Viet Cong are trying to do! You retarded muthafucka," said Sharon, in her best Vera imitation.

Charlee was temporarily flabbergasted, but he heard Sharon loud and clear. He was stuck and reliving his worst nightmare: being trapped in darkness. He knew, Sharon knew, he hated the two factors. Quickly, he regained his footing as his psychological prowess began to play tricks on him. The darkness turned into a hot dark, Vietnamese jungle filled with hidden armed Viet Kong. Sharon's voice turned into a Vietnamese dictator on a bullhorn urging Charlee to give up information or die. He chose to fight. Like second-nature, Charlee dove behind the same pillar he had just run into. For now, it was a bush and his only cover. He was back in Nam and in the trenches.

"You'll never take me alive muthafucka!" He yelled as an imaginary assault rifle appeared in his hands. Sharon laughed so hard she feared her stomach would burst open, as she left the house to find her mother.

Sharon loved the sights, sounds, smells and sheer thrill of the urban night life. Every step she took was a step into the almost forbidden unknown variant an impoverished inner-city night life had to offer. She absolutely loved the dangerous mystery of the night. Trotting innocently to find her mother on Broad Street, Sharon noticed that she was near a fence that housed a ferocious German Shepherd. The dog sent chills up her young spine. Cautiously, she crossed the street to avoid the mongrel, but as she crossed the middle of the street, she frightfully observed that the fence was wide open. Before she could figure out if the dog was present, a terrible snarl gave her a clear, unmistakable answer. Within seconds, the large dog was closing in on her. Sharon took flight as she weaved in and out from between parked cars. Try as she might, she could not totally break away from the dog who was gaining ground on her. In a last-ditch effort, Sharon darted into the street and narrowly missed getting slammed into by a speeding car. However, the dog, was not so fortunate. The speeding car not only hit the dog, but kept on speeding and totally ran the dog over as it let out a painful howl. The out-of-breath Sharon smiled, the feeling of victory lanced through her young, wicked heart, as an idea took over her brain. Quickly she ran back to the accident site and studied the dead dog that was sandwiched to the concrete asphalt. Amazingly, the dog still held onto life by a thin thread. Sharon cocked her head to the side at the sound of the dying dog's sorrowful whimper. Another sudden idea caused Sharon to quickly produce a small pocket knife she usually carried around. It was a gift from Charlee. She stared the animal in the eye and stabbed it until it whimpered no more. The feeling she felt at the exact moment when she took the animal's doomed life was so thrilling that she silently vowed to feel it again and again. Sharon was so delighted and excited that she licked her small pocketknife and tasted the still warm blood.

"Must taste like Charlee," she mumbled to herself, as an oncoming car beeped her out of her insane trance.

"Sha-ron! Sha-ron! If you don't get your crazy ass from up out the street eating a muthafuckin' dog! Bitch I feeds you! You ain't Chinese! Get your ass out the street," wailed Vera.

THE SHARON SLAUGHTER STORY

She was a passenger in the very car whose movement Sharon was obstructing. Sharon found the sidewalk as Vera continued to yell.

"Where the fuck is Charlee? You out here eating a muthafuckin' dog! Where is he?" Sharon pointed towards the house as Vera scooped her up by the arm and whisked her to the house. Inside, Vera sentenced Sharon to the kitchen as she yelled out for Charlee. Hearing no response, she began to look around the house, starting upstairs. As soon as Vera reached the top of the stairs, Sharon took action. She ran to the locked basement door and opened it.

Peering into the darkness of the basement, she yelled, "You traitor, I'm sending in forces!" in a husky voice before slamming and relocking the door. The sound of Vera coming down the stairs sent Sharon flying back to the kitchen.

"What? Who said that?" barked an angry Vera.

Sharon laughed as Vera unlocked the basement door and turned its light on. Before Vera could react, Charlee grabbed her, covered her mouth and rolled down the basement stairs.

"I'm Charlee! You Charlie! Damn Cong! Acting like you Uncle Sam! You ain't no damn Sam! I got your ass! Come to my world," ordered a deranged Charlee while holding onto Vera for dear life.

Sharon's heavy laughter and the basement's light caused Charlee to snap out of his temporary insane fi t. Vera crawled and wrestled her way out of his grip to make it off the ground and to her feet.

"Char-lee! Char-lee! What the fuck! You better stop that tripping shit! Retarded muthafucka! If you broke my muthafuckin pipe I'ma kill your retarded ass! I swear before Christ," ranted Vera, as she kicked Charlie and checked her pocket for her brand-new pipe.

Satisfied that her pipe was intact, she quickly produced a sixteenth of the new and exciting party drug, crack cocaine. Vera had, only moments ago, turned her first trick and secured the product. She had also just mere minutes ago tried the drug and loved it and she wished for Charlee to try it also.

Vera broke off a tiny section of the narcotic and stuff ed it in the pipe as she lit and inhaled the fumes like the veteran that she was. Vera held onto the smoke for dear life not letting a single vapor escape. She gave Charlee a no-look pass of the pipe and implored him to do the same. He obliged while still sitting on the floor. As the rock sizzled in the pipe, Charlee broke out in a sweat as he felt his spirit leave his body, heading towards Vera. He inhaled the smoke as he watched a phantom version of himself choke Vera. Confused, Charlee blew out the smoke and tried to repeat the process, but Vera snatched the pipe and lighter from his hand. While this happened,

Charlie's apparition of himself disappeared like crack smoke. Vera lit and sizzled another rock before she ordered Sharon to close the basement door. This was to be an all-night affair.

Sharon awoke still seated by the closed basement door. The intense growling in her stomach made her open the basement door against her mother's wishes. Venturing down a few steps, she could clearly see her mother and Charlee searching the basement floor intently for something. Interested, Sharon made her way fully down into the basement to see what the search was about. In an honest effort to join the search, Sharon was verbally assaulted by her now irrationally impaired mother.

"Oh no! No! No! No! Sharon get your little fast ass from down here. You probably done stepped on the rock! Give me your muthafuckin' shoes and get back upstairs!"

Sharon did as she was told, yet, halfway up the flight of steps she screamed of hunger. Vera dutifully ordered Charlee to fix Sharon a meal while she continued to look for rock. Famished himself, but in more need of the rock, Charlee humbly obliged. Joining Sharon on the staircase, Charlee turned to address Vera, only to see her searching the bottom of

Sharon's tennis shoes with intense concentration. He held fast to his comment and exited the basement. Charlee had a plan to not only feed Sharon but to find more rock by any means necessary. His new addiction would be the guiding post of his life. Today would mark the beginning of that troubled journey and Sharon would be his faithful accomplice.

"Sargent Sharon front and center!" announced Charlee to Sharon's delight.

"Get your sandals on and meet me out front in three minutes!"

Sharon laughed as she quickly equipped herself with her rubber sandals and met Charlee outside. She stood in front of Charlee in an almost perfect attention stance. Charlee paced back and forth with his eyes never leaving the concrete ground. A plan was formulating in his mind as he imagined the city transforming into Vietnam.

"Sargent Sharon were on ah…ah, ah, ah a spec, spec, special re, re, re, re, recon, ah, ah, ah, recon mission. To ah, to, to recover umm, um, um to recover food, ah, ah, ah to recover food rations and ah, ah, ah, rock! Fo, fo, fo follow mmm, mmm, my lead!" he said as Sharon held back a laugh. Suddenly, without warning, Charlee marched off into the burning summer sun. Sharon absentmindedly followed him without question. Many painstaking minutes later, Charlee stopped his march and picked up a hand-sized piece of metal that he found perfect for his plan. Not too far from this, he decided to hide in a garbage filled alleyway where he discussed his plan with Sharon.

Sharon waltzed into a Korean variety store beaming with cheer as she methodically collected a number of items she loved to consume. As planned, she took her time and gathered everything her heart desired. Content, she placed the items on the counter and began her performance. She threw herself to the floor and shook her body like an epileptic suffering a violent seizure. The lone owner of the store, a middle-aged Korean man, raced from behind the counter to aide her. Upon this sudden chain of events Charlee appeared behind the store owner with a shirt wrapped around his face and metal in hand. He calmly placed the metal against the store owners back.

"Do ah, ah, ah, don't, ah, ah, ah, mo, mo, mo, move muthafucka! Wa, wa, wa, wa, walk ova, ova, over-"

"Don't move! Walk over and empty the cash register and pack the groceries Charlie!" interrupted Sharon helping Charlee.

The surprised store owner was so frightened that he flagellated on the way to the register. Yet, he managed to obey all the orders Charlee was barking from behind while staying out of his line of sight. When the store owner announced he was finished, Sharon collected the bounty and fled to the selected "rally" point in Charlee's plan. With the plan almost complete Charlee walked the store owner over to the canned food section of the store. Feeling a crude ending was near, the store owner begged for mercy. Ignoring his pleas, Charlee hit the store owner in the back of his head with a large sized can of baked beans until he lay unconscious. Charlee then fled the store with speed knocking down two incoming store patrons.

Back at Charlee's "rally" point, which was the middle of a garbage riddled nearby alleyway, Charlee tallied up the proceeds. The total take was for four hundred and twenty-three dollars and Sharon's momentary food cravings, which included three boxes of cereal, one gallon of milk and a host of candy and snacks. Sharon loved her first act of crime and begged Charlee to let her be an accomplice on many more capers. Charlee smiled but neglected to give Sharon a direct answer. However, with money in his palm, the strong bellowing of addiction took control of Charlee's mind. He had to find the rock now. He ordered Sharon to meet him back at "HQ", he had yet another "recon" mission to complete.

Everyone was "Charlie" to Charlee: the police, the drug dealers, even a stray dog was Charlie. So, on this hot humid morning, Charlee's mission was to avoid Charlie and find the rock at all costs. He figured this could be accomplished by staying off the main street and using a series of alleyways until he reached narcotic central, 8th and Butler. He may have been new to the rock genre but Charlee was sure he could find it there. On so many nights, he had heard Vera speak of the narcotic activity that took place there. The talk excited him and he dreamed of experiencing the location. Today was his day and he would make the best of it. Leaping and scaling all matter of dirty, disgusting items, he made it to the location in a very short amount of time. He could taste the sizzling rock inside his mouth, all he had to do was find it. Stepping onto Butler Street, he was shocked at the large volume of foot traffic. Drug addicts went to and fro in a steady stream. It reminded Charlee of a bizarre. He didn't know which way to turn. With anxiety pumping through his veins, he decided to ask a mobile drug addict.

"Ah ah ah sa sa say, ah ah ah sa sa say, say ma ma ma ma man."

His efforts were futile and he grew hungrier for the rock. Retreating to a nearby alley, he once again covered his face with a shirt and brandished his trusty piece of metal. He intended on watching the busy street corner until he could see an opportunity to seize the rock. He didn't have to wait long, for in the in the mist of stealth, he witnessed a young narcotic dealer hide his stash not too far from himself. Charlee was beside himself with happiness, he decided to wait until the dealer came back to his stash, to apprehend both the dealer and the stash. In the blink of an eye the dealer returned and was quickly subdued and relieved of his stash and currency.

Charlee beat him unconscious with his bare hands. With the mission complete, he made his way back to "HQ".

Sharon bothered Vera not, for she had a variety of perishable items to consume before Charlee returned. She knew that upon his return, he would have whatever her mother was still looking for on the basement floor. In her young mind, curiosity of the elusive item plagued her thoughts. If only she could just see what it was. With a mouth stuff ed full of candy she watched from a living room window as Charlee marched up the street towards the house.

"Mama! Here Comes Charlee!"

Hearing Sharon's announcement, Vera continued her basement floor search physically, yet her mind prayed Charlee had more rock. Charlee entered the front door drenched in sweat. His bottom jaw shook due to the purity of the cocaine the rock contained. He made three pit stops to sample the rock before arriving home. It was of the fi nest quality Philadelphia had to off er. So much so, Charlee had escaped his body and retreated to a lost in time space in his mind, every time he took a deep a deep blast of the pipe. The advanced euphoric feeling had in fact increase his libido, thus lust was the only reason he came home. He was hell-bent on invading Vera's rectal cavity. His eyes wandered the living room as he encountered a grinning Sharon who said nothing. She merely pointed toward the basement and continued to laugh. Charlee moved swiftly towards the basement with Sharon's plight for traps fi rm in his mind. Entering the threshold of the basement, he slammed the door shut and made it down the stairs to an agitated Vera. Charlee took off his shirt and produced a handful of rocks. Vera promptly snatched them out of Charlee's hands and stuff ed two into her pipe. Charlee stood back against the wall and watched as Vera elevated her spirit into the realm of temporary utopia. Slowly, Vera broke out into a sweat as she tried to recapture that blissful escape of reality the next two vials of rock had to off er. Charlee removed his boots and pants silently. His eyes never left Vera. The sizzle of the rock made her sit down as she held onto the fumes in her nostrils. The lack of oxygen supply to her brain gave her a slight feeling of vertigo. Charlee removed his underwear as he himself lit his own pipe and let the rock sizzle. Instantly, he transformed into a wild tiger both in mind and body. Vera, now stuck staring at her fingers, didn't even notice Charlee lurking behind her. Like the tiger he thought he was, Charlee pounced on Vera and ripped her clothes off. Vera yelled in fright, powerless to stop him. Hearing the commotion, Sharon cracked the basement door to see what the fuss was about. What she witnessed was a drug-induced Charlee ram his undersized penis into the depths of Vera's anus. At first, Sharon thought to rush to Vera's aide. However, upon hearing Vera's pleasure filled grunts and acquiescence, Sharon realized something she never before laid eyes on. Her mother and Charlee were having sex. Twisted and sick as it seemed, Sharon shut the basement door and tried to make sense of what she saw. This was her first impression of sex in real time. It would have a profound impact on her sexuality for years to come.

Months had passed with Sharon observing the same routine; Vera and Charlee rotating in and out of the house in hard-earned eff orts to retrieve the rock. The elusive rock. Sharon had yet to lay eyes on the popular, in-demand item. But today was a new day, a day for adventure. Sharon vowed to lay hold of the rock and at least see what it looked like. Her plan was set in motion as soon as Vera left the house to pursue her prostitution career. Charlee, as usual, worked in another area of the house. Unattended, Sharon slipped out the back door and through a small alley. It was midday and the streets of North Philadelphia were alive with lewd behavior. Loud raucous music blared from every direction; people yelled all manners of obscenities while drinking heavy intoxicants as fresh dog feces littered the ground. Sharon walked wide eyed as she took in her dubious surroundings. She carried nothing but the thrill to see the rock. Sharon searched and searched until she found herself on Broad Street. The boom of city life paralyzed her motion. She was caught up in the rapture of the amalgamation of people. In her transient daze, she saw Vera at work peddling flesh. Alarmed, Sharon took refuge behind a newsstand where an idea appeared in her mind. She would follow Vera to the rock. Hiding out of sight, she watched as Vera strutted up and down Broad Street in vivacious apparel, chasing car after car in hopes of securing a "trick" for income. Sharon barely managed to keep up until, at last, Vera was waved down by a walking customer. This excited Sharon, for she knew that once currency touched Vera's hand she would find and purchase the rock. She followed Vera and "trick" into a nearby side street alley, where Vera serviced the man from her knees in seconds. Hiding behind a large, foul-smelling dumpster, Sharon watched the entire ordeal and to her credit, she also managed to follow the pair out the other side of the alleyway. It was there that Sharon watched Vera make a subtle transaction.

"The rock!" Sharon exclaimed under her breath in a fit of excitement.

From her vantage point, she could see two jumbo vials with red tops. As she made an eff ort to continue following Vera, her path was obstructed by a friendly cat. Surprised, Sharon lost sight of her goal and focused on the cat. Bright fawn and white, the raggedy street cat purred softly as it rubbed up against Sharon's legs. Another idea invaded Sharon's thoughts. With devious hidden intentions, she quickly picked the cat up and found her way back home. There she managed to smuggle the cat inside without alerting Charlee. Locked safely inside her room, Sharon retrieved a cache of hidden, quarter sticks of dynamite left over from Independence Day. Cautiously, she fused several sticks together into one fuse and place the lethal row around the cat's neck. It resembled a crude collar. The dastardly deed was almost complete, she only needed a means to light the connecting fuse. In a dash, she managed to steal Charlee's lighter and lock herself back in her room. Satisfied, she didn't hesitate to light the connecting fuse.

THE SHARON SLAUGHTER STORY

Boom! Boom! Boom! Boom! Boom! Boom! Boom!

Each blast blew a chunk of the cat's head spiraling into the air. The sound of the quarter sticks of dynamite also sent Charlee crashing into the floor. His mental capacity told his conscious mind that he was back in Vietnam and under fi re. Like an animal, he scurried along the floor until he made it to Sharon's door. Once there he burst through the locked door to find a gruesome macabre scene. At first glance, he thought Sharon was injured. However, her wicked grin silenced that thought. "Sh sh sh Sharon! Ah ah ah ah what ah ah ah th th the hell!"

Sharon broke out into a mad laugh as she marveled at her room's decor.

It had been weeks since Sharon's quarter sticks of dynamite fiasco. It was now school season. Despite being a prostitute and a drug addict, Vera had managed to not only register Sharon in school, she had also secured her proper clothes and school supplies. Sharon, on her first day of second grade, looked the part. In school, she excelled in all of her courses, but history was her favorite, especially stories about Native Americans. She loved to hear the brutal tales about how the Native Americans practiced warfare against the invading Caucasians. After setting into several weeks of school routine, Sharon was approached on her lone walk home by a man claiming to be her father. Weary of strangers, Sharon shunned the man and bolted home believing she had shook the man off her trail. Moments later, the same man knocked on the front door, putting out that theory. Charlee answered the door and immediately recognized the man. It was Lonnie, a steady "trick" of Vera's that refused to go away. Actually, Lonnie was not a "trick", he was, in fact, Vera's boyfriend, before Charlee. Vera informed Charlee of the false pretense to hide Lonnie's role in her life as a "sugar daddy" and Vera's "get high partner". Vera had often lied to Lonnie about the location of her living quarters to avoid a confrontation between Lonnie and Charlee. But one fact that Vera did reveal to Lonnie was the fact that Sharon was indeed his daughter- a fact that Charlie was completely in the dark about. But on this day, Lonnie would not be denied. He was determined to meet his daughter and take her and Vera with him.

"Charlee move! I'm taking my daughter and Vera with me muthafucka! So you better move out my way," barked Lonnie as he pushed Charlee aggressively. Charlee pushed back and stood his ground. Sharon watched in delight as the two men fought for dear life. As Lonnie began to get the upper hand, Vera appeared in the front door and hit him in the back of his head with a nearby living room vase. More startled than hurt, Lonnie turned to face Vera.

"Bitch you coming home with me and my daughter!"

Before Lonnie could strike Vera, he was stabbed in the side by a bloodthirsty Charlee. He continued to stab Lonnie with his small pocketknife until Lonnie fled the house. Sharon laughed a horrid chuckle at the incident until her stomach hurt. She was promptly struck by Vera and told to go to her room. For Vera and Charlee had a date with the rock.

The winter season was in full bloom which meant absolutely nothing in the drug world. It was just a cold day, but a cold day filled with just as much narcotic activity as a summer day. Except that this day was a sort of family day for Sharon and company. Vera and Charlee had just attended a Thanksgiving Day play in which Sharon starred as a disgruntled Indian. The play, as well as Sharon's role in it was successful. To celebrate, Vera and Charlee promised to take Sharon to the local variety store for her to get her fill of a few select items. Once they arrived, the Korean owner immediately recognized Sharon from the robbery he fell victim to that past summer. To further confirm his suspicions, the sound of Charlee stuttering sealed the deal. As Charlie approached the counter, the owner produced his newly acquired fi rearm and fi red. POP! POP! POP! Charlee's brain matter littered the faces of Sharon and Vera. Shocked, Sharon licked her top lip and tasted Charlee's thoughts.

Charlee's sudden manner of death shocked Vera so much, she had to be committed to a mental institution. All she could manage to do was stare at the small piece of paper that the head nurse had given her so many years ago and mumble. If it wasn't for Lonnie, Sharon would have become a ward of the state.

The transition from Vera's custody to Lonnie's custody was easy for Sharon. She found solace inside of herself, deep within her own reality. It had become normal for her to hold entire conversations with herself. She even had an imaginary friend named Sheila. Sheila was primarily responsible for many of Sharon's wicked thoughts, or rather, Sharon held her responsible.

Sharon experience something new in Lonnie's care; fear. Sharon truly held fear in her heart of Lonnie. She had good reason, Lonnie was not only a drug addict but a mean-spirited alcoholic who believed in beating her furiously with a belt. His narcotic of choice was "crank", which he poured into his beers on a daily basis. Lonnie, unlike Vera, was against crack cocaine. Despite his narcotic abuse, Lonnie was actually a good father in his own twisted way. He enrolled Sharon in a private Catholic School in their new residence, Northeast Philadelphia. There he maintained a well-paying construction job, for; he was a classic "functioning addict". In this seemingly average scenario, Lonnie paid little attention to the dangerous psycho Sharon was growing into.

1992

Sharon was now sixteen years old and a student at Northeast High School. She had convinced her strict, rigid father to take her out of Catholic school by way of constant begging, or so she thought. Unknown to her, Lonnie began to worry that Sharon would become "crazy like her mother" as he put it. This was due to the fact that on numerous occasions he had overheard her having long, drawn out conversations with herself. Lonnie had hoped that the change of scenery at school would open Sharon up to a more normal social life. He had no way of knowing his daughter would meet her lifelong friend and the absolute worst influence any parent could imagine.

It was the first day of school for Sharon and she was excited. Though her style of dress was not of the norm, (Sharon dressed with a Native American influence) she was well put together to say the least. Making it through her first few periods of classes, the thought of lunch and a cafeteria overrun with people she knew not, frightened her. So she decided to walk the school grounds outside and explore what the neighborhood had to offer. But first, she needed a quick visit to the bathroom. As soon as she opened the bathroom door, her nose was assaulted by the stench of a lit cigarette. Not knowing who she was, the cigarette was quickly put out by one of three older female students. Shyly, Sharon put her head down and tried to pass them.

"Bitch, why you got feather earrings and a blanket on for?" said a light skin female with freckles, as she blocked Sharon's path. Sharon tried aimlessly to get around the female, but it was of no use. The young woman would not be ignored. The other two females surrounded Sharon, now she was trapped from behind.

"Bitch, I said why you got on feather earrings and a muthafuckin' blanket?" cornered, Sharon decided to answer.

"Cause I like Indians! Now can you please move! I gotta piss!"

The three females broke out in a hyena like laughter as they gave Sharon her wish. Sharon entered a stall and relieved herself. But as soon as she opened the stall door, the obvious leader of the pack once again approached her.

"You cute little bitch, what is your name?"

Sharon, a bit caught off guard, answered without thought.

"Sharon."

"Well ok, my name is Kitty and these are my two homegirls, Saundra and Rachel. I ain't never seen you round here before, so you must be new. We bout to go to Sandra's aunt's house to hang out and drink Taylor Port. You trying to hang?"

Sharon wanted to say no but Shelia made her lips move and pronounce yes. Kitty led the way as the all-female group of four promptly left the school grounds. The entire journey Sharon listened as Kitty told tales of sex, drugs, and a subject Sharon never encountered before, lesbianism. The very mention of the lucid topic excited her. Once they reached their destination, Sharon noticed that there was no adult supervision. She took a seat and a drink as she watched the other three females unwind in loose, raucous fashion. In this atmosphere, the females, mainly Kitty, questioned Sharon about her background. Sharon divulged everything about herself, minus Shelia and her thirst for carnage. One fact she did express was her quest to see what "the rock" looked like. Kitty quickly stopped dancing and disappeared into an upstairs room for a short spell.

When she returned she held a large freezer bag filled with jumbo vials, with red tops. With no care, she threw the bag on Sharon's lap. Sharon inspected the vials with amazement.

"These are really just tiny rocks! My mother and her boyfriend used to go crazy over these! Wow!" she said in fascination.

"Girl niggas is getting large off that shit! My home girl Rasheeda stole them from some nigga she was fucking. I'm just holding it for her until my homie Paula can sell it for us," responded Kitty as she gyrated her hips to the loud music.

Sharon put the bag down, got up, and danced in imitation of Kitty. The more the Taylor Port took effect on Sharon, the more Sheila controlled Sharon's actions. Two hours in and Sharon was really enjoying herself. She was visibly drunk and now half dressed. Kitty saw this and took advantage. She escorted Sharon up to her room and closed the door. Kitty invited Sharon to lay on her bed. Sharon obliged, even though she was nervous. The Taylor Port and Sheila made her bold.

Without notice she forcefully kissed Kitty.

"Wait hold on girl! Shit! I guess I ain't got to do much coaching with you! You ready huh? Ok bitch slow down let's take it one step at a time. Ain't no rush I live here with Sandra and her aunt. Her aunt ain't gonna be here for a while, she working, relax," said Kitty taking control. Sharon laughed in nervous tension as Kitty produced her well-rounded breast. At the mere sight of Kitty's breast, Sharon on instruction from Sheila, bit Kitty's left breast with a slight tone of aggression. *"Oww! No Bitch! Too hard! What the fuck is wrong with you?"* said Kitty in extreme dismay.

The look in Sharon's eyes made kitty put her shirt back on. This action by Kitty made Sharon come on to her more aggressively. A slight wrestling match ensued and Kitty was the victor. On top of Sharon, Kitty managed to shove three of her fingers inside Sharon's vagina. Sharon howled in pleasurable pain. Before Kitty could go any further, another female barged into the room.

"Damn Kitty! Where the work at? I found a nigga that can move it! You in here playing and shit," said the intruder in an irritated tone. Kitty relinquished her hold on Sharon and exited the room with the intruder. Sharon laid back on the bed and listened as Sheila instructed her to use a lighter located on the nightstand to set the window drapes on fire. Normally, she would have been able to resist Sheila's wicked suggestions, however, under the influence of the Taylor Port, Sharon couldn't help herself. She seized the lighter and lit the drapes. As the flames grew she stood back and admired her accomplishment.

"Bitch, what in the fuck," announced Kitty as she snatched the flaming drapes down and stomped

out the fire. The look Kitty once again saw in Sharon's eyes told a wild story.

'*I gots to keep an eye on this lunatic bitch*,' Kitty thought to herself. Sharon began to dance in a very seductive and wild fashion. She was having the time of her life. That merry time was cut short by an annoyed Kitty.

"You going to have to dance your crazy ass outside somewhere else! I got shit to do Sharon, I will see you at school tomorrow bitch!"

Sharon found Kitty in the exact same location as the previous day. Kitty even elected to leave the school grounds early, same as she had the day Sharon met her. Sharon was elated, however her joy was temporary, due to Kitty's ready-made plans.

"My home girl Paula gonna pick us up and we gonna hang in North Philly," announced Kitty as she and Sharon gracefully exited the school grounds.

Sharon was in fact looking forward to a day filled with lesbian behavior and acts of debauchery. Kitty noticed the look of disappointment painted across Sharon's face.

"Don't worry girl shit will be fun! Paula gonna have some Taylor Port and we might see some fly ass niggas out North!" ranted Kitty.

Sharon was confused, she truly believed Kitty was solely a lesbian. The mention of males did pique her interests. Right on schedule, Paula beeped the horn of her beat up 1984 ragtop Chrysler LeBaron. The loud horn caught Kitty and Sharon's attention immediately. The two quickly entered the vehicle as Paula pulled off. Paula gave Sharon a curious once-over before commenting.

"Ok Kitty I see you got your little friend with you huh?"

Kitty and Sharon shared a bashful glance as Kitty turned the radio up in an obvious attempt to change the subject. The all-girl group jammed to the music while passing around a once full bottle of Taylor Port. Kitty gave Paula directions until they ended up in North Philadelphia on Colorado Street. Sharon vaguely knew the area. It was Kitty's neighborhood and she knew not only the landscape, but the people as well. Per Kitty's advice, they sat on the vehicle and carried on their drinking affair. After a spell, the group was approached by a small crowd of reckless males in their same age range. All the males knew Kitty, some even knew Paula, however, Sharon was a hot new addition. Taylor Port clouded the young females' judgment, for they made the bad decision to join several of the young males in a nearby rundown house to continue drinking. A few hours in, all three females had split up and were each partnered up with a male counterpart in different sections of the house in private. Alone with a male, Sharon found herself half-naked and on her knees with a penis in her face. The Taylor Port silenced any inhibitions Sharon might have had. Sheila took control. Placing the penis in her mouth as she had seen her mother do on so many occasions, Sheila told Sharon to "do what came natural". Sharon chomped down on the young man's penis with all her might. This action caused the tip of the penis to be completely severed from the shaft and land in Sharon's mouth. The young man let out a blood-curdling howl, so loud the entire street heard his pain.

Sharon spit out the tip as Sheila forced her to laugh. To Sharon the penis tip tasted nothing like steak or Charlee. The injured young man fainted in shock. Kitty gained her senses and rushed Paula and Sharon out to the vehicle as she commanded Paula to drive. Paula totally inebriated managed to side swipe the entire block before she got control of the vehicle Sharon laughed throughout the ordeal.

Sharon hated when her father took her to visit her mother. She longed to see Vera in her former state. On those difficult visits, Lonnie wouldn't even physically see Vera, he would merely take Sharon, and wait outside the room until Sharon would leave. So on this particular visit, Sharon assumed it would be along those lines. Sheila thought otherwise. Sharon smiled shyly as Lonnie took his regular seat at the door. Out of the corner of Sharon's eye she saw Sheila (who looked exactly like Sharon) lighting a fi re in a small trash can. Sharon ignored Sheila. In her mind anything that she imitated of Sheila got her in trouble. She focused on the feeble Vera who sat mindless in front of her. Vera's hair was unkempt and she wore standard hospital-patient garbs that the mental hospital changed from time to time. What didn't change was Vera's possession of the small piece of paper she had received from the head nurse when Sharon was born. The paper consisted of a name (Sharon) and a phone number. Nurses had made many attempts to seize the paper. The results always ended in Vera suddenly coming to life and raising hell until the paper was returned to her. So today as Sharon did Vera's hair, Sheila tempted Sharon to not only burn the paper, but also Vera, by lighting the fumes from a can of hairspray. Try as she might, Sharon could not continue to ignore Shelia. The temptation was too great. Sharon began to spray Vera's hair with a very generous amount of oil sheen. She did the same with the small piece of paper. Using a lighter, she sprayed the flame with oil sheen and ignited not only Vera's hair but, also the small piece of paper. Vera yelled out in pain but her only concern was the paper. Lonnie rushed in and quickly put out Vera's hair. The paper was destroyed and so was the key to keeping Vera stable. Vera kicked and screamed as the attending staff tried to calm her. It was of no use, Vera had to have the small piece of paper more than she had to have hair. She fought the staff like a wild animal until she was silenced by sedatives. Sharon claimed the fi re was an accident. Sheila had won yet again.

Sharon found herself home alone. There was no school so she couldn't meet up with Kitty in the bathroom. Sheila convinced Sharon to walk to Sandra's house to find Kitty. Sharon found herself a bit lost along the way, yet she still managed to find the house. Knocking on the door, she was greeted by a rather large female.

"Fuck is you?" said the female as she looked down at Sharon.

Sheila told Sharon to bite the tall female, yet Sharon opted to ignore her.

"My name is Sharon and I'm looking for Kitty cat," said Sharon innocently. "Let her in Roxanne 'fore the bitch bite you," said Kitty from inside the house.

Roxanne obliged. Sharon entered the abode and found it relatively full of young women.

"Kitty how old is she?

"She cute!"

"She don't look crazy."

These were the chants Sharon walked into.

"She's 16 y'all relax! Sharon have a seat. We having a meeting! This all my home girls! We ain't got no name or nothing shit. We just kickin' it! Let me introduce you to everybody. Y'all this is Sharon. Sharon you already know Sandra and Rachel. The tall bitch that let you in is Roxanne. This right next to me is Rasheeda, I was telling you about. And you, oh I forgot! You already know Paula over there," barked Kitty the obvious leader.

The young females present, ages ranged from 16 to 21. They discussed everything from men to female empowerment. Sharon was in a daze. She believed she had finally found a place amongst a group of her peers who accepted her for her. The entire time the young women chatted away, Sharon said little. For she fought the urges to act out what Sheila was whispering in her ear. It seemed all the young women ever spoke of was sex, narcotics and money. Being the youngest in the room, Sharon only found sex interesting to a certain degree. Her intentions in coming to Sandra's abode were to drink

Taylor Port and explore her taste in other women. Sharon was so far removed from the conversation she didn't even know she was the topic.

"Sharon! Sharon! Bitch hello! Do you hear me? If you trying to be down you gotta change your gear and set a nigga up for us. You down?" urged Kitty with aggression.

Sharon nodded in agreement not really knowing what gear was or setting somebody up really meant.

"Good good! Ok little bitch here is the plan."

Sharon walked awkwardly in the high heels Paula had equipped her with. The heels came along with a short mini dress, a tight-fitting halter top and a full face of makeup. Sharon loved her new attire, it reminded her of the Vera of old. That was the image she tried to emulate in her mind. Silently, Sharon wondered what Sheila thought of her new look. This endeavor marked a maturity in her mental health capacity. She no longer thought of Sheila as an imaginary friend, she now referred to Sheila as a defiant part of herself, an "alter-ego" so to say. With every step Sharon took forward, Sheila began to surface and take control. The giddy nervous young Sharon was gone. Sheila was here to complete her mission. Her task was to get close to Tim, a 25-year-old crack cocaine trafficker who had laid eyes on her in the mist of the Colorado Street fiasco. He had been targeted by Kitty and company many months ago, yet no one in her circle could get close to him. His interest in Sharon spelt a twofold opportunity for Kitty. One, her group now had a means to not only learn, but rob Tim's lucrative operation. And secondly, if the plot was successful, Kitty would gain a new member for her group.

So on this chilly fall day, Sharon walked back and forth in front of her school as she waited to get picked up by Tim. She had been prepared well for her mission by Kitty. All that was expected of her was to gain inside information on Tim's operation and relay that information to Kitty and company for a review of the best possible way to rob Tim's booming narcotic business. As Sharon practiced her walk, the loud boom from a thunderous sound system caught her attention. It was Tim driving a 1992 Volvo station wagon, gold in color. He rolled down a tinted window and locked eyes with Sharon. Her seductive wear gave him an immediate erection. He signaled for Sharon to join him. Her eyes darted in the direction of Kitty and Roxanne who hid in a nearby car. Kitty gave her the okay and Sharon joined Tim in his vehicle. As soon as Tim sped off with Sharon, Kitty and Roxanne followed closely behind.

"So you go to Northeast High huh? That's wassup, I went to Gratz," said Tim as he studied Sharon's figure from the corner of his eye.

Sharon only nodded as she also studied Tim. He was fairly skinny, very light complexion and had curly black hair. He wore a Reebok windbreaker sweat-suit, Reebok Pump sneakers and several gold chains. Tim looked the part of a typical inner city drug dealer. Sharon was indeed attracted to him.

'*Bite his muthafuckin cheek off Sharon and see how it taste*,' Shelia chimed in Sharon's head. Sharon ignored Sheila as she tried to make small talk.

"Yeah umm, I like Char- I mean steak. Fried steak! What do you like to blo- I mean eat?"

"Oh so you hungry? We can swing on up to Sizzlers up 69th street and grab a grub," responded Tim never taking his eyes off Sharon's legs.

The ride was awkwardly silent the entire trip except for Sharon periodically mumbling commands to keep Sheila silent. Tim's silence was due to his slight fear of Sharon. He constantly thought of the Colorado Street scenario and what could become of his own penis.

At the restaurant, Sharon showed off her hidden talent, eating. She gorged herself plate after plate until she could barely move. Tim was amazed at her ability. He was correct in thinking of bringing Sharon to a buffet. Tim was also correct in his approach to not rush Sharon into sex for surely Sheila would have manifested. He only politely, dropped Sharon back off in front of her school and promised to be there again tomorrow. Even though Tim offered to take Sharon home, she was ordered not to let Tim know where she lived. Kitty reasoned that if the robbery attempt went bad, it was best that he didn't know where Sharon lived for fear of retaliation. Walking home, Sharon was picked up by Kitty and Roxanne. She changed her clothes in the car before heading home.

"Good job so far little bitch! You might turn out fi ne," complimented Kitty as they drove to Sharon's house.

Weeks had passed and Sharon had been dating Tim at a regular pace. He had showered gifts on her and taken her everywhere except around any of his narcotic haunts. And most of all, Tim had yet to try any attempt to have sex with Sharon. The plot she was assigned to carry out was getting nowhere. It was now the beginning of October and Kitty and company had grown restless.

"Sharon you going to have to give that nigga some pussy! I know you said you was a little virgin and all but bitch if you want to earn this niggas trust you gonna have to give it up! Especially if you trying to be down with us," barked Kitty. "Plus, we got a few niggas that Sandra and Rachel fuck with that will tie Tim scary ass up," she continued.

Sharon sat in the midst of Kitty's circle a bit torn and lost in thought. It was on the one hand, the very first time Kitty's idea and Sheila's demands matched. On the other hand, Sharon was afraid to lose her virginity to a man. As Kitty went on and on Sheila could take no more.

"Bitch I'm gonna eat that nigga Tim for breakfast! Next time he slide through his ass is mine! Imma eat him alive! He will tell me everything!" Sharon blurted out in aggression.

The shocked woman stared at Sharon in fear. Paula was the first to speak out.

"No no! No more of that! We trying to get info from the nigga not kill him! Crazy ass muthafucka! Just get him somewhere and get him comfortable and let Sandra and Rachel's dudes tie his ass up! He will tell them what we need to know."

The young women in attendance seemed to all agree with Paula's logic. Well, all, except Sheila. She ranted and raved inside Sharon's head until Sharon silently agreed to follow Sheila's plans when the time was right. Out loud, however, Sharon agreed with Paula. The plan was set for that very night. Tim planned on taking Sharon to her new favorite hangout; Chinatown.

Sharon was ecstatic at what she had found in a small knick-knack store in the heart of Chinatown. The location of the date was Tim's idea. He'd gotten the idea from Sharon's constant raving about Asian culture. Once they arrived in Chinatown, this particular store caught Sharon's attention due to the various odd-looking gadgets in the display window. In particular, it was the array of specialty knives.

Dressed to the tune of a provocative streetwalker, Sharon peppered the store owner with a million questions as Tim heard and saw nothing except Sharon's profound frame. The sting of lust was too great for him to ignore. That night, he planned on probing Sharon's vagina with expert precision. A question from Sharon caught his immediate attention and made him think of her chomping past.

"Wow! And you say Vietnamese women used a blade device similar to this one to skin the penis of American soldiers in Vietnam mister?"

Tim immediately interrupted the dangerous banter and made up an excuse to exit the store before Sharon could get any ideas. Angry beyond belief,

THE SHARON SLAUGHTER STORY

Sharon physically showed no sign of emotions yet inwardly she let Sheila take control. Walking back to the short-term parking lot where Tim's car was parked, Sheila made Sharon seductively engage a surprised Tim. He tried in vain to hide his erection inside his fitted Guess jeans. Sheila zeroed in on the bulge and made Sharon grab it with just the right amount of force. The grope nearly caused Tim to explode in an orgasm on the spot. His rational thinking went out the window. He made his way to his vehicle quickly and informed Sharon that they were headed to his house with speed. Sheila caused Sharon to laugh out loud for Tim was, indeed, about to have the time of his life. The entire ride, Sheila caused Sharon to sexually tease Tim in every way imaginable, as he raced at double the speed limit. All the while, he prayed she wouldn't devour his penis, literally. Unknown to the lustful couple, they were being followed by Sandra, Rachel, and their two armed, muscle-bound boyfriends. The plot was conceived by the female group out of Sharon's earshot. They didn't trust Sharon's ability to employ the proper decisions to find out information on Tim's narcotic business.

Tim arrived at his Overbrook Park abode just as Sharon began to slightly undress. He quickly whisked her into the house and joined her in undressing. Seeing a penis so close frightened Sharon. Sheila on the other hand was excited to say the least. She made Sharon get down on her knees and try to swallow

Tim's entire penis. This cast out all worries Tim had about Sharon feasting on his penis. Sharon tried to get a grasp on the situation to remember exactly where she was so that she could relay the information to Kitty and company, but Sheila wanted penis down her throat in an eff ort to gain Tim's trust. Sharon argued slightly with Sheila, which caused Tim to wonder what she was babbling about with his penis in her mouth. Just as Sheila had convinced Sharon to bite off Tim's scrotum sack, a knock at the door interrupted them. Both Tim and Sharon wondered who it could be. Tim eased away from Sharon and maneuvered impatiently through the dark living room before carelessly opening the front door, eager to dispatch the intruder so he could get back to getting pleasured. A large figure suddenly appeared and with a vicious swing sent Tim sailing through the air. The sudden action frightened the naked Sharon and she struggled to find her clothes as a light came on. Two large burly figures glared at her with a look of part contempt and part lust.

"Damn sweetheart put your clothes on! Ol' boy out cold so your part is done! Sandra and Rachel outside waiting so go! We got this from here! We gonna take this nigga car home! Hurry up!" said one of the huge men.

Sharon obliged and joined Sandra and Rachel outside in a dash.

"Bitch can you believe that nigga Tim was living with his Mama! That fucking car wasn't even his, it was his Mama shit to! Cold fronting! Working for somebody else! Roc-Roc and Bam say he ain't have no money, only vialed up crack and a bunch of weed. They kept the weed and gave us the crack. Dumb ass niggas! Crack worth more! But we gonna use they big asses for muscle! Said they knocked Tim ass right on out and tied him up like it wasn't nothing! We need them niggas!" yelled Kitty at the room full of females.

Sharon laughed with the group. Sheila, on the other hand, was furious. She disliked the way the ordeal transpired without her being in control. The more she got involved with the group, the more she wanted to run things and replace Kitty as the leader. Sheila's thoughts boomed inside of Sharon's head so much she started to develop a headache. Her struggle to control Sheila inside her head caused her to mumble to herself frequently, so much so Kitty noticed.

"Sharon! Sharon! Girl fuck is you mumbling? You down with the clique now and you didn't even have to give up the pussy!" announced Kitty, making Sharon smile. "Girl here drink this Taylor Port and party with us! We got another nigga for you to jux! It will be easy girl, Imma go with you," continued Kitty as she passed a bottle of Taylor Port to Sharon.

As soon as Sharon took a sip of the strong brew Sheila took control of her mind and body. Jumping on top of the large living room table in one swift leap, she ordered the other females to turn the music up louder and watch her. She gyrated her pelvis in such a slow, seductive manner that all the females shared a shocked glance. One by one, she flirtatiously danced with each of the girls in the room. She urged them to rub up against every curve on her young body. The raunchy performance stunned everyone in attendance. By the time Sharon got control of Sheila it was too late. Everyone in the house knew she had a wild side to her quiet character, in a way, Sheila had become a member of the group as well.

Embarrassed by Sheila's last fiasco with the gang, Sharon decided to break off from the group for a brief moment, in an eff ort to find a better way to control Sheila. In doing so, she found herself wandering the crime-riddled streets of North Philadelphia. Late afternoon turned into night as she realized she was now lost in the Hunting Park section. At this hour, only the lost souls of perdition roamed the streets in search of feeble means of existence through immoral acts. Little did Sharon know she would soon be a victim of one of these acts. As she found herself close to the park for the third time, a young male who must have been roughly around her age started talking to her and learned that she was lost. To Sheila, he was a skeeming vermin, not worthy to live. But Sharon blocked out Sheila's thoughts and followed the youth to his house so she could use his phone to call her father. The youth directed her to a dilapidated house a stone's throw away from the park. Inside, Sharon found the house full of males, youths and adults. They stopped shooting craps when Sharon appeared. They all shared anxious glances as the front door was locked and Sharon was led into an upstairs back bedroom. The innocent youth disappeared and he was replaced by several other young men in a flash. Sharon was then beaten and raped by at least nine males. During the ordeal, Sheila waited in glory, for she loved to be beaten forcefully and taken against her will. Sharon, on the other hand, felt abused and filthy. Afterwards she wandered the streets until she found her way home and was once again beaten by her father and pronounced a whore. From that moment on Sharon vowed to live by the crude, abrasive and vile thoughts of Sheila. She would only be Sharon in name. The very next day she went back to the very same house where she was raped and robbed of her virginity and had sex with all the males again and again until they gave up and the experience lost its thrill. Sheila was in full control.

1993

;m. Sharon found herself straying further and further away from not just home but school as well. She also avoided contact with Kitty and company, Sheila had forbidden any further contact with the group. She urged Sharon to venture out into the world on her own. Sheila allowed Sharon one pleasure of her own and that was long visits to the Philadelphia Free Library. There, Sharon studied and researched various topics ranging from Native American cultures to natural poisons. The library was her safe haven. The solace she found in the quietness of the confines of the information within the establishment gave her an escape from reality. After a few weeks of solitude, Sharon began to only go home to shower and refresh herself. She totally stopped attending school. It seemed that the massive amount of information she stockpiled in her mind had silenced Sheila for the time being.

As winter turned into spring, Sharon found herself a part of a homeless community that resided around Love Park. When nighttime took over the city, living outside made her feel like she was having the Native American experience. Back at home, Lonnie had made a missing person's report to the local authorities. Sharon was clueless about this fact. She merely never went home and lived, off the fat of the city. But her life would change abruptly one fateful morning as she was panhandling in downtown Philadelphia at the main entrance to the Gallery Mall.

"Oh my fucking God! Sharon is that you looking like shit?" bellowed a surprised Kitty in the company of Paula.

Before Sharon could answer, Sheila drowned her thought process and took over her being.

"Well hell the fuck lo to you too bitch! How 'bout I chew the side of your face off while I paint my toenails?" answered Sharon in dark humor.

Kitty and Paula shared a nervous laugh for a brief moment before Sharon joined in the laughter as well. Taking in the scene, Sharon noticed Kitty was adorned in gold jewelry and glowing with glee. Her gold bamboo earrings had her name engraved on the inside and this caught Sharon's attention. Paula on the other hand was also dressed to kill. However, Sheila could smell fear protruding from her person. Before Sharon could question Kitty's giddy persona, Kitty quickly elaborated on her happiness.

"Girl I got a new dude named Chronicle and he a little younger than me but let me tell you! He is so fucking large! Remember Rachel and Sandra's boyfriend Roc-Roc and Bam?" Sharon nodded as Kitty continued. "Yeah he they hommie! He used to go to the high too girl! Oh shit I forgot."

Kitty's face changed dramatically in an instant and Sharon was puzzled.

"Somebody found Rachel in a crackhouse dead. She overdosed on pills and Sandra got hit and ran over by a fuckin' car girl. Fuckin crazy shit," said Kitty, putting on her absolute best actress performance.

Sheila burst out laughing in Sharon's mind but Sharon's face showed concern.

"Girl I've been back and forth driving Chronicle out of town. Him and his little friends is in this little hick town called Williamsport getting paid! A lot of shit done went down! I will fill you in on the way to our spot out the county. You down or what?"

Sharon took a brief second to rationalize the thought in her mind. She really enjoyed living on the fringes of society. On the contrary, Sheila feigned for excitement, Sheila's desire won the battle.

"Yeah gurl I'm down by law! Together we some real La Femme Fatale bitches!" Sharon blurted out in bold fashion.

Kitty and Paula shared curious glances. They liked the way La Femme Fatale sounded but didn't know what it meant. Obvious to this fact Sharon clued them in to the meaning.

"It means like dangerous or lethal women."

Due to Sharon being an illegal runaway, she was ordered by Kitty to stay indoors within the group's abode until they could figure out a formative plan. She quickly found herself bored with the sheltered life and turned to Sheila for the excitement of adventure. All of Sheila's ideas seemed to revolve around either harming her roommates- Paula, Rasheeda and Roxanne- or setting something on fi re. Amazingly, Sharon managed to ignore Sheila's promptings but they came to a sort of compromise and agreed on a horrible act, finding small animals and not only torturing them but mutilating and scalping them in the ways of the Native Americans. The animals would serve as a substitute for human victims for the time being. Sharon went about this task in the wee hours of the morning dressed in Native American fashion, complete with face paint and traditional head-dress. All she had in her possession was a surgeon's scalpel, an anatomy book and a small pouch filled with cat food. She reasoned that cats would be the only plausible animal she could find. The sun had not yet risen, and Sharon dutifully found Main Street, trekking along the path until she found herself on MacDade Boulevard in Collingdale, PA. After an hour of walking, she had yet to find a cat. Frustrated, Sheila convinced her to return to the house and slit Paula's throat while she slept. Tired, Sharon agreed and made the journey back home and into Paula's room in stealth. Silently she watched as Paula slept peacefully. Sharon quietly produced the scalpel and thought of a proficient way to slash Paula's throat without making any noise.

'Bitch just cut her motherfucking throat, she can't scream without a voice box' yelled Sheila in Sharon's head.

"I am! Will you just wait a second? Damn!" responded Sharon out loud awakening Paula.

The sight of Sharon dressed in Native American regalia, holding a scalpel close to her throat, caused Paula to scream in horror. Her shrieking awoke the entire house. Roxanne and Rasheeda came to the scene in a fit of confusion.

"What the fuck is you doing Sharon? Fuck you got on!" questioned Roxanne in an aggressive posture.

Rasheeda merely stood in the doorway in a state of shock. Sheila had to think for Sharon fast.

"Paula was talking in her sleep. I thought somebody was in here hurting her! I came to help fast as I could."

Paula, Rasheeda and Roxanne all shared disbelieving glances before Paula chimed in.

"This crazy bitch was trying to slit my fucking throat! Oh my God what the fuck is wrong with you?! Get the fuck out my room! I'm getting a gun!"

Roxanne escorted Sharon out of the room, while Rasheeda did her best to calm Paula down. After a few tense hours, they all found solace in the living room eating a magnificent breakfast prepared by Paula. Often when Sharon and Paula would lock eyes, Sharon coached by Sheila, would make a grotesque face in an eff ort to tease Paula. From that day on, Paula never trusted Sharon and whenever she slept in the same house with Sharon, Paula slept with the door locked shut and a makeshift weapon within arm's reach.

Kitty would often come to the hideaway and tell tales of crime and passion which always centered around her boyfriend Chronicle. On this particular visit, she brought the women gifts specific to each one's style and character. For Paula, she brought a money counting machine because she envisioned Paula being La Femme Fatale's treasurer. For Roxanne, she bought a shotgun because Roxanne was to be La Femme Fatale's security. For Rasheeda, she bought an illustrious gold chain because Rasheeda was the glamorous attraction of the group. And for Sharon, Kitty brought a set of Japanese blades because Kitty saw Sharon as a "wildcard" of the group, their secret weapon. Sharon loved her handcrafted blades. She would practice throwing them at a wall in her room. Kitty also brought major life-changing news; she was pregnant. With this stark revelation, Kitty told a tale of her boyfriend/babyfather stalking a man and not only killing the man, but also his nephew and newborn baby. The room was shocked into a stunned silence until Sharon, coached mentally by Sheila, broke out into a hideous laugh.

"3 in one huh? Damn ok Kitty got yourself a killa huh? Ok girl," said Sharon in a deep blunt voice.

The entire room shared nervous glances. It was crystal clear that Sharon was a raving lunatic. Kitty broke the eerie silence by getting to the matter at hand, her real purpose for the visit.

"The summer bout to come y'all and you already know it's La Femme Fatale season! Now since the JBM done went down last year, everybody wanna get a piece of the muthafuckin' pie! Now my dude and his crew got Larchwood on lock! Plus they be outta town and they took over some shit they call the Backstreet down in the 50's. I say we join forces with them niggas and get our piece shit! What y'all think?"

The room broke out into a fit of yelling.

"Kitty fuck them niggas! Let's get our own shit!"

"Do we gotta fuck em?"

"Do Chronicle got a brother?"

"How much money they got? Let's rob them niggas!"

Sharon didn't understand what was going on. She wasn't privy to the politics of the underworld. She could care less. All she and Sheila wanted to do was cut flesh with her new blades. As the females argued and bickered Sharon abruptly got up and left. Once again, she went on the hunt for a cat to butcher. While she was gone, Paula secretly called the authorities and conveyed Sharon's whereabouts and her runaway status. Sharon was apprehended and returned to her father.

"You been missing for months! Doing God knows what with God knows who! What in the hell was you doing walking down the damn streets of Darby with God damn Chinese knives!" Roared Sharon's father as he savagely beat her with a belt buckle.

He hit her so hard the blows caused Sharon to urinate on herself in fear. She crashed to the floor and lay in the fetal position to protect herself.

"You ain't shit but a streetwalker like your damn mother!" Lonnie continued, as he beat her to a rhythm.

His last statement struck a chord deep within Sharon and awoke Sheila. Instantly, Sharon began to laugh and she regained her footing. Confused, Lonnie tried to swing the belt harder. It had no effect on Sharon. She merely laughed as she inched closer to him. Now nearly face-to-face with him, with Lonnie being only a bit taller, Sharon lunged up at his face and chomped down on his nose. She held onto it with all her might and will. Lonnie screamed, but try as he might he could not escape Sharon's bite. After several painful seconds of struggling, Lonnie managed to free himself from Sharon's grip with half his nose missing. Wailing in pain, he fled the house and spilled into the street. Seeing an opportunity to flee herself, Sharon hot-tailed it to her room, packed a few bags and used the phone to contact the La Femme Fatale lair. Luckily, Kitty was present to answer the phone, she guided Sharon to a safe zone where she could pick her up. After this incident, Sharon's father contacted the proper authorities and reported Sharon as once again being a runaway, with the intention of having her jailed until she was an adult.

Spring turned into summer as Sharon's character annoyed her roommates at the La Femme Fatale's hideout. Paula, in particular, was totally uncomfortable with Sharon's presence. They were all especially annoyed by Sharon's horrid singing. Sharon had recently grown obsessed with the sultry singer Sade. Her room walls were littered with posters of the famous singer. Her obsession was so intense she had styled herself to look exactly like Sade, or so Sheila thought. Sharon's mental health during this time also took on a new form. When speaking to any of her roommates, Sharon would sometimes, in mid-conversation switch the topic to whatever Sheila urged her to speak on. Also, on numerous occasions, the roommates listened in secret as Sharon had intense, full-blown conversations with Sheila in the privacy of her room. They urged Kitty to rid them of Sharon to no avail. Kitty believed she had a special purpose in the group.

One fateful summer morning Sharon eavesdropped on a conversation between Kitty and Paula that intrigued her in every way.

"Girl, Chronicle don't even know I'm pregnant! I don't want to stress him out right now cause he done fucked up! Girl he owe that crazy Voodoo bitch Mamai Lucia a half million dollars!" hollered Kitty in full animation. "And," she continued. "You know the bitch kidnapped Bam and Tone to make Chronicle come to her! And guess what?"

"What? Kitty tell me girl."

"That bitch was cutting up a fucking body as she told Chronicle what time it was."

At the very mention of a human body being mutilated, Sheila made Sharon go down to the living room and participate in the conversation. She was in fact so invigorated she nearly fell down the stairs on her way to the living room.

"Mamai Lucia who? Tell your dude to break us off with some of that cash and I will dice that bitch up and eat her for breakfast," announced Sharon in bold fashion, influenced by Sheila.

Kitty and Paula shared a shocked glance for a brief moment before Kitty shed light on the situation.

"I knew this little bitch was crazy! I knew it! I knew it! I knew it! Muthafuckas can't tell me I ain't no psychic! How about I got a better idea? How about we let my dude pay the bitch then we kill her and take the money? Fuck asking a nigga for shit! You know what La Femme Fatale say?"

"Pussy make the world go round!" the room chanted in unison.

Kitty and Sharon sat in Paula's 1984 ragtop LeBaron outside a dilapidated string of row houses in the Badlands section of Philadelphia. The purpose of the trip was to get a visual on Mamai Lucia. Kitty knew of the woman's lore, it carried on from the Badlands to the Kensington section of Philadelphia. Kitty's own mother would often seek out Mamai Lucia's domestic and spiritual help, yet Kitty never laid eyes on the legend.

"Gurl Mamai Lucia got a whole bunch of houses from here to Kensington. Word in the hood is, she right up the street here. I still can't believe she into drugs, but Chronicle swear on everything so I believe him. Speaking of Chronicle, gurl don't you know we had to get his ass from Larchwood yesterday! Nigga smoked some wet and tripped the fuck out!" said Kitty as the two erupted in laughter.

Kitty went on to explain the ordeal as they kept their eyes trained on the target house. Minutes turned into hours and they had still not seen Mamai Lucia.

"I don't know, Kitty, maybe she ain't in there. Let's go and knock on the door. Shit, let's just ask for her."

Kitty ran Sharon's suggestion through her mind for a moment before deciding against it. She had another plan.

"Nah nah not just yet Sharon. Let's go down to Love Park. It's dark outside I got another idea. I wanna make sure you ain't like Sandra or Rachel soft asses."

The mention of Sandra and Rachel made Sharon frown her face in curiosity. Kitty noticed the look and responded immediately.

"What you frowning for huh? Listen, let me tell you a little secret between us."

Kitty reached under her seat and produced a firearm before she continued.

"Sandra and Rachel wasn't La Femme Fatale! Them bitches was soft! I couldn't risk them turning my baby daddy and his crew in! I had to do it! And guess what? We gonna go down to Love Park and find somebody, anybody and you gonna kill them! Ain't nobody gonna miss no fucking bum! But here is where the shit get real at Sharon. If you don't kill one of them bum muthafuckas, I'm gonna do you! And that's word to fuckin' Big Bird! You hear me?"

Sharon, controlled by Sheila, looked Kitty directly in the eyes for a second in eternity before she broke out into a hideous laugh. The laugh made Kitty a bit uneasy as she put away the firearm and pressed on the gas pedal. The entire ride to Love Park was marked by Sharon's horrid singing. Kitty turned up the music in a futile effort to block out Sharon's voice. Once the pair arrived at Love Park, Sharon, ever so anxious, tried to exit the vehicle even before Kitty could fully park.

"Bitch wait a minute! Now sit yo crazy ass still while we go over the plan. Listen this what we gonna do. We gonna find a random bum nigga, front like we gonna give him some pussy, take his ass somewhere and you gonna smoke him with this gun. Got it? It can't be somebody you know 'cause I don't want you to freeze up cause you too familiar. Ok." ordered Kitty as Sharon looked her in the eyes like a giddy school-girl.

She smiled happily as she nodded in agreement. As the two exited the vehicle, Kitty had a sinking feeling in her stomach that she just couldn't put her finger on.

'Either this bitch crazier than a muthafucka or she is stupid ass little weird bitch. Either way tonight, I'm gonna find out,' Kitty thought to herself.

BLACK MAMBA

Walking into the park, Kitty was taken back by the sheer volume of people that were in attendance. Sharon led the way as they scouted for a potential victim. She was vaguely familiar with a few people, none of which fit the bill for extermination. Kitty felt totally out of place. It was apparent that Sharon would have to pick the victim. Forty-five minutes into their search, someone stuck out. His name was Touch and he was known in the homeless community as a rapist and abuser of homeless women. He was exactly who Sharon was looking for. He had made a number of explicit overtures toward Sharon when she lived in the homeless community. On one occasion, Sharon had to literally fight off one of his advances. She whispered into Kitty's ear that he was indeed the proper target. She also informed Kitty that she was familiar with him. Kitty tried her best to convince Sharon to pick a more unknown random target but Sharon was hell-bent on proving herself. Conceding to Sharon's demands, Kitty played along with the plot perfectly. Touch followed Kitty and Sharon to a vacant alley where they positioned themselves beside a large trash dumpster. As soon as Touch pulled his pants down Kitty produced her firearm like magic. She then gave the firearm to Sharon. Laughing, Sharon gave the firearm back to Kitty. Furious, Kitty trained the firearm on Sharon.

"Bitch I told you if you frog up I'm gonna kill you! I'm gonna kill you and this raggedy ass muthafucka," roared Kitty in seething anger.

THE SHARON SLAUGHTER STORY

Touch looked from Sharon to Kitty in a state of shock mixed with fear. His penis went from stiff to flaccid in an instant. Laughing, Sharon went into her pocketbook and produced one of the Japanese blades Kitty had given to her as a gift. With a sudden lunge and a few swift hacks, she managed to slit Touch's throat, striking a major artery in his neck. Gasping for breath, Touch fell to the ground and died a slow agonizing death. Still laughing, Sharon waltzed over to his body and cleanly hacked off his lifeless penis and put it into her pocketbook. Kitty held back vomit as she fled the scene. She made it to the vehicle in the blink of an eye while Sharon skipped in glee. Kitty yelled at her through the vehicle's window in an eff ort to quicken her pace. While leaving the area at top speed, Kitty shared her thoughts.

"Bitch don't tell nobody I ran! We gonna keep this shit here a secret between us!"

Paula, Rasheeda, Roxanne and Sharon listened intently as Kitty brought them news of the latest happenings. In fact, Paula only half listened. She silently brewed heavy with envy and jealousy because Kitty, for some strange reason, seemed to be favoring Sharon. As Kitty broadcast her juicy gossip, Paula would ever so often cut her eyes at Sharon.

"This stupid ass nigga just busted in the house and started blasting! I got a few fuckin' pellets in my fuckin' arm! If only Chronicle ass knew I was pregnant! I backed his stupid ass up! Oh, did I mention his flow in Williamsport is still booming! Jumping! Clocking paper! He got two bitches up there getting it! And I know he fucking both of them! Wait..." buzzed Kitty as she flopped down on the sofa in silence.

She was now in deep thought.

In the silence, Sharon in a child-like manner imitated the shoot-out Kitty had just finished speaking of.

"I would have smoked that old bitch Kitty! BAM! BAM! BAM! Oh shit Kitty, guess we can get that money from Mamai Lucia now that your dude at war with her! Shoot! Dang," rumbled Sharon breaking the silence.

Kitty nodded in agreement before she stood up and made an announcement.

"Pussy make the world go round! Pack your bags bitches we gonna go up to Williamsport to pay them bitches a visit! Fuck that! Roxanne, Rasheeda and Paula, y'all up! We gonna see if y'all La Femme Fatale material!"

The trip to Williamsport was marked by heavy marijuana smoking and Sharon's terrible singing. No one was more bothered than Paula. She wondered why everyone was to be tested except Sharon. Added to that fact was Kitty and Sharon's new apparent bond. It was painfully obvious to everyone that they shared an unseen, tangible understanding that allotted Sharon a "special" place in Kitty's confidence. Whatever that understanding was, each of the other three females vowed to themselves to reach that same goal.

Three hours into the ride, the group arrived in Williamsport and quickly found Wilson Street. Kitty parked a few houses down from Megan's house and turned the vehicle off.

"Kitty what the fuck is we doing in this hick ass town? We ain't got no work or shit to do," barked Roxanne as she exited the vehicle to stretch her legs.

"Fuck the work! And we got something to do! Now get back in the car bitch before somebody see you," instructed Kitty in a show of dominance. Roxanne begrudgingly followed her orders. Kitty then explained everything before tempers flared.

"Now we up here cause these low life bitches is getting my man's money and more than likely fucking him. Now I'm not gonna lie. Driving up here, I was mad as hell. I wanted to come up here and kill both these bitches and rob them. But sitting here in this hick town, fuck that murder shit. We gonna rob this white bitch and beat the dog shit out of the black little bitch he got in the projects up here. I know my man; he might have got a dick suck from the white bitch but he ain't fuck her. He wouldn't fuck no snow bunny! But the black bitch with the fat ass! He fucked her! I know it! I've been in the house with the white bitch, but when he get money from the black, funky ass bitch, he always go alone or with somebody from his little crew. So I know what's up! But I saw the house she live at in the little townhouse project shit called Timberland or something and I know how she look! I even heard Zero say the bitch be in this little bar, deli type shit across from her house called the Shamrock. So here is the plan…"

Roxanne, Paula and Rasheeda knocked on Megan's door in anxious fashion. The sun had just set and darkness covered Wilson Street. After several knocks, Megan's mother Jill answered the door and was greeted with the barrel of a .357 Magnum.

"All the money is in my daughter's room I swear!" cried Jill as Roxanne pushed the fi rearm in her temple and forcefully moved her back into the house.

"Take me there bitch! Don't look at me!" barked Roxanne.

As Jill led the way to Megan's room at gunpoint, a rail thin man appeared at the top of the staircase. The man was visibly intoxicated and very brave. He dove down the staircase in a valiant but failed effort to attack Roxanne. She merely slapped him alongside his skull with the butt end of the pistol. The blow knocked the man out cold. During the action, Paula and Rasheeda stood paralyzed in fear.

"Matter of fact, bitch tell me exactly where it's at so my home girls can get it!"

"Under the mattress!"

"Y'all heard her! Go get that! And hurry the fuck up! "

Paula and Rasheeda darted upstairs and retrieved the cache of currency, hurrying out the front door without waiting for Roxanne. To make their exit easier, Roxanne hit Jill in the back of her head with the butt end of the pistol, knocking her out cold as well. The three females made it successfully to a nearby alley where Kitty and Sharon were waiting and they all fled into the night.

Forty-five minutes later, the group sat on West 4th Street close to the popular bar-deli, The Shamrock. Anxiety and adrenaline from their latest caper still bubbled in their stomachs. They were on a roll and Kitty truly felt the power of being in control.

"One down one to go! Sharon walk me to this Shamrock shit so I can see if we can spot this bitch! If she ain't in here we gonna walk to her house and stomp a mudhole in her ass!" said Kitty as she and Sharon exited the vehicle.

Paula sucked her teeth in jealousy while Roxanne took control of the driver seat.

Kitty and Sharon made it to the Shamrock quietly and searched it without locating Lisa. Following the plan, the duo found themselves in the Timberlands housing complex at Lisa's front door. With each knock, Kitty grew angrier, for she pictured Chronicle coming through this very same door each time he had sex with Lisa. Finally, after several tense moments, Lisa appeared in the doorway in a fi t of anger.

"Word yo! Who the fuck is you knocking at my fucking door like you the police bitch!"

Sharon responded with a swift swipe to Lisa's face with one of her Japanese blades. At first, it seemed as if Sharon's gesture missed its mark, however seconds later Lisa's face revealed a six-inch razor-thin gash that sprayed out blood as she tried in vain to back away. Kitty rushed forward and unleashed a fury of hate filled blows that eventually floored the wounded and stunned Lisa. Fighting from the floor on her back, Lisa kicked and screamed for her life. Hearing the struggle, Lisa's children came to her aid and were easily kicked away by Sharon. Fearing Sharon would butcher the children, Kitty quickly ushered Sharon out the house and back into the vehicle.

The group made away with thirteen thousand in cash and the scuffle left Lisa requiring seventy stitches across her face. Megan didn't believe her mother was robbed. She attributed the loss to one of her mother's schemes. Thankfully, the lost currency was hers and not a payment meant for Chronicle. Lisa thought her attackers were in fact a different group of females who she had a previous scuffle with. In either case, Chronicle knew not, of La Femme Fatale's involvement.

Sharon was ecstatic about her latest progress in the group. She had also, of late, been seeing eye to eye with Shelia, or rather, their thoughts had been in sync. It appeared to Sharon that the more violent and unpredictable she acted, the less she had to deal with Sheila. So it was on this bright summer morning that

Sharon and Sheila agreed to take Sharon's take from the Williamsport raid (a hefty $2,500) and splurge on it in Chinatown. Borrowing very provocative attire from Rasheeda, Sharon trekked to the Darby Loop, caught the 11 trolley to downtown Philadelphia and walked happily to Chinatown. Two hours into her trip, she had managed to spend almost half of her proceeds. Satisfied with her purchases, she found her way home and locked herself in her room. Her roommates listened attentively as she engaged in a full conversation with Sheila, about what to do with her new catalog of knives. Or rather who to use them on. Besides knives, Sharon had also purchased Asian apparel and a plethora of books that covered various topics from feudal Chinese warfare to poisons 101.

As day turned to night, and night into the wee hours of the morning, Sharon was awakened by the sound of a yelling and highly agitated Kitty. Sharon exited her room and entered the living room where she could see all of her roommates surrounding a frantic Kitty. She sat on the staircase and listened as Kitty ranted and raved on in an emotional tangent.

"This bitch Mamai Lucia is fucking crazy! She cut off Chronicle's momma's head and left it in our house! I can't fuckin believe it but I seen it! I just dropped him and his crew off at Larchwood! This war shit is on for real! Oh my fuckin God! This bitch know where we live at! What the fuck am I supposed to do I'm fuckin pregnant! Oh my God!"

THE SHARON SLAUGHTER STORY

Kitty ran up the stairs past Sharon and right into the bathroom where she vomited in the toilet. The entire house sat in silence as Kitty sobbed. Sharon was speechless but Sheila had something to say. Standing in the middle of the living room, Sharon expressed Sheila's thoughts.

"Pussy make the world go round! I say we get close to this Mamai Lucia bitch and cut her fuckin' head off! She only know Kitty and Chronicle's team. She don't know me! Y'all ain't got to do shit but get me close and I will gut the bitch like a fish!"

Silence once again filled the air as everyone present except Kitty wondered whether or not Sharon's words were true.

"I don't know Sharon this bitch sound looney! Plus you keep talking this killa shit! Who the fuck you even kill bitch! You hype as shit," said Paula in an attempt to deflate Sharon.

Sharon inched closer to Paula, so close Paula could smell Sharon's breath. "I would have slit your throat bitch if you ain't wake-up," whispered Sharon through clenched teeth.

Roxanne broke the two up as Kitty took a seat next to Rasheeda. Kitty and Sharon shared a curious glance that made Paula wonder what secrets they shared.

"Sounds like a plan! But we gonna have to act fast cause I know my nigga! Him and his crew gonna be on the hunt for that bitch! So we gotta come up with something. In the meantime, I'm a see what Chronicle thinking about doing so we can move accordingly. What you think Rasheeda? You always quiet! Doing your nails and shit. Girl this shit serious! What you think?" said Kitty as all the attention shifted to Rasheeda.

"Control Chronicle's crew and keep us the best kept secret. Whenever you see an opportunity, we should be on that before them. Pussy make the world go round!" said Rasheeda as she stood up and gyrated her hips. The room erupted in laughter; however, the laughter was only a nervous reaction to the severity of the situation.

"Get dressed let's go kill that bitch Mamai Lucia!"

"By myself?"

"No stupid, I'm with you."

"What about Kitty and the gang?"

"What about them bitches? They ain't like us!"

"But we in a gang!"

"Fuck the gang! We a gang! We really run this shit!"

"No, Kitty the leader."

"Bitch you sound like a cheerleader!"

"I like Kitty."

"More than me?"

"No, but she did a lot for me!"

"Bitch if we kill Mamai Lucia we get all the glory!"

"But Sheila I don't know how she even look."

"Just get dressed! We going to that house Kitty took us to! We can start there!"

Fortunately, Sharon's loud conversation with Sheila was not overheard by anyone due to the empty La Femme Fatale hideout. Following Sheila's instructions, Sharon dutifully got dressed with stolen attire from Rasheeda's room and caught a series of SEPTA transportation standards to the exact location Kitty had taken her previously. Sharon was hesitant to knock on the door. Checking her purse, she made sure she had a "special" acutely sharpened stiletto. Gathering her bearings, she knocked on the door and waited in silent trepidation. Moments later, a tall, elegant woman answered the door. Sharon was taken back by her size and beauty so much so that she fumbled around trying to find the right words to address her.

"Ah ah yeah I'm uh uh, I'm here to see Mamai Lucia."

The tall woman cocked her head slightly to the side before answering.

"She does not reside here at the moment. But if you have any spiritual needs I can see you right now."

Sharon was intimately perplexed about the notion of having a spiritual reading. After all, she had no formal religion. In fact, the only religious experience she'd ever had was attending a Catholic school. Still, Sheila urged her to proceed with the reading so she could truly see if Mamai Lucia was present or not. Sheila also reasoned that if Mamai Lucia wasn't present, killing the tall woman would be a consolation prize.

"What you mean like tell my future?" she said like a giddy school-girl.

The tall woman laughed as she moved aside so Sharon could enter the home. Stepping into the house, Sharon casually reached into her purse and clutched her stiletto tight. She was ready to maim at a moment's notice. Taking in the sights, she silently wondered what a fortune teller 's house was supposed to look like. This house was as plainly furnished as any house she had ever seen. The tall woman led her down the stairs to a dim lit basement. Refocusing her eyes, she noticed that a corner of the basement was elaborately laid out with a number of tureen vessels that were decorated with different colors. Some were placed on the floor while some were arranged high on bookshelves. Sharon was clueless as to what they contained.

"Please put your purse and belongings on the chair in the far corner to the left. After that, please cover your chest and midsection with this white sheet. Oh I almost forgot! Please remove your sandals and place them at the bottom of the stairs, then join me here on the mat," the tall woman instructed as she sat down on the other side of the mat with her back to a wall that held a number of the Tureen vessels.

As soon as she sat across the mat from the tall woman, the hairs on Sharon's body rose like she had stuck her finger inside an electrical socket. She felt an imminent sense of awareness that neither her nor Sheila could fathom. Her face showed nervousness and apprehension.

"Relax! There is no charge and I promise you that you will be greatly informed on your life as it is and how it shall be."

The tall woman's words soothed Sharon but made her much more anxious to get through the process and hear the results. Just then, the tall woman began to sing in a language Sharon cannot understand. As she sang, the tall woman produced a set of seashells that she asked Sharon to hold. Moments later, she took the seashells from Sharon and cast them onto the mat. Sharon watched as this mysterious woman studied the shell's patterns and wrote something down. This procedure was copied several times before the tall woman made her revelation.

"Your reading is strong and definite. I see you are fighting for control of yourself from within. You have a new family that one day you will be the mother of. Your name shall be spoken of in fear. Be aware, my friend, the spirits say an enemy posing as a friend will threaten your position. Love for you, will come in time, upon a common thread."

Sharon was so astonished at the tall woman's revelation that she regained her footing, grabbed her purse, and bolted out the front door leaving her sandals behind and totally abandoning her plan.

Sharon was in a state of constant paranoia. The tall woman's accuracy concerning her current life was mindboggling to hear, and her prediction for the future also seemed to ring true. She thought about everything the tall woman said over and over again.

Sheila explained everything to Sharon in her own interpretation: Fighting for control of herself was letting Sheila control her totally, Sharon being the mother of a new family was Sheila running La Femme Fatale, which Sheila felt was already happening. Sheila felt that Sharon's name would be spoken of in fear if she just listened to Sheila all the time, and love for Sharon coming upon a common thread was sharing mutual thoughts and actions with Sheila. The one part of the revelation that Sheila couldn't explain was the primary cause of Sharon's paranoia, which was an enemy posing as a friend threatening her position in the group. Neither Sharon nor Sheila could figure out which of her roommates could be the enemy. For all of her roommates seemed to not like Sharon. Kitty was the only person in La Femme Fatale that Sharon would consider a friend. Kitty was also the obvious leader of the group and this fact alone made Sheila suspect that Kitty could be the enemy. Who else would challenge Sharon's rise but Kitty? Sharon paced the floor in her room repeatedly as she mumbled in low tones to avoid any of her roommates hearing her conversation with Sheila.

"Sharon it's Kitty!

"No Sheila Kitty really is my friend! We have that secret!"

"Secret? She has dirt on you and as soon as she's ready to get rid of you, she will turn you over to the police."

"Sheila just shut up and stay out of my business."

"I am your business Sharon!"

"Sheila—"

Sharon's mental collapse was cut short by the sudden appearance of Kitty.

"Sharon who the fuck is you talking to? What the fuck is you doing walking back and forth? Gurl, Mamai Lucia done shot up Chronicles mom's funeral earlier today! I just dropped him and his crew off at Larchwood! I told him I had to run to the store because I don't want him to know about our spot yet until this shit is over! I just came to check on y'all," said Kitty in a worried tone.

Sheila was doing cartwheels in Sharon's mind.

'Kill her Sharon! She ain't come to check on you! This bitch was eavesdropping on our conversation! Kill her! Kill her! It's a blade right behind you in the nightstand!' ranted Sheila in Sharon's mind. Sharon mentally fought off Sheila's urges while her body backed up closer to her nightstand. Kitty continued to voice her concerns as she took a seat on Sharon's bed. She was in perfect striking position for Sharon.

"Gurl I just don't know right now. This shit is getting deep. It's like I have to worry about

Chronicle's crew and y'all. This nigga and his crew is crazy! I know they ain't gonna stop until they kill that bitch or she kill them! Plus, Chronicle talking 'bout killing his little foster brother's connect and taking over his shit like he don't already got enough shit on his plate! It's like I got to think for his wild ass! Oh and not to mention I'm horny and pregnant and he won't even fuck me! Stupid ass black muthafucka still don't know I'm pregnant! But right now, I'm running the show! So what you think?"

Sharon sat on her nightstand and secretly opened the top drawer slightly enough to reach in and retrieve the blade.

"I don't know Kitty, it sound like a lot of shit going on," said Sharon as she secured a Japanese blade secretly with her right hand. Before she could act, the room was suddenly filled with the remaining La Femme Fatale members who joined Kitty on Sharon's bed. Outnumbered, Sharon dropped the blade and pretended to be attentive to the growing conversation.

"It is a lot of shit going on but I got a plan. I'm gonna use one of Chronicle's boys to get close to somebody in Mamai Lucia's camp, maybe even Mamai Lucia herself," said Kitty full of pride.

Everyone in the room acknowledged Kitty's brilliance except Sharon. She merely nodded her head in approval as Sheila's thoughts ran rampant in her mind.

'See that bitch think she Queen shit! Look Sharon! Look how they all are ganging up on you! They here to kill you! Bitch pick up the blade and at least get Kitty first! Kill! Kill! Kill!'

Sharon shook her head in a vain eff ort to stop Sheila from invading her mind. It was of no use. Sheila would not stop until Sharon took action. As Kitty and the other La Femme Fatale members continued to engage in conversation, Sharon bolted out of the room in madness. Her inner fight had reached a boiling point and she needed to be alone before she yielded to Sheila's demands. For the time being, her temporary refuge was the basement of the house where she locked herself away in darkness until Sheila's thoughts subsided. All of the members of La Femme Fatale just thought the pressure of the current events made her a bit uneasy which triggered her odd actions. Little did they know her odd actions may have saved their lives.

Sharon awoke from a deep sleep on the basement floor. Her body ached from the concrete floor she used as a mattress. The dark damp basement felt like a place she could retreat to within her mind, a place she could explore without outside interference. With little thought, she began to look around the basement. At first, her search only yielded her miscellaneous items such as a beach chair, old children's toys, and holiday furnishings. However, upon further searching Sharon found a cache of pornographic material. The obscene material contained a plethora of articles from pornographic magazines and revealing pictures of a former tenant of the house. The graphic images lit an animal hunger inside of Sharon and strangely enough, Sheila remained quiet. A particular image of a female with her own fingers buried inside her vagina caught Sharon's attention. The way the woman's posture arched in pleasure as she maneuvered her fingers in and around her vagina captivated Sharon. So much so, Sharon pulled down her tights and underwear and mimicked the images. The feeling she felt sent electricity through her body. As the sensation blossomed, violent images of bloodshed and ghoulish debauchery flashed in her mind. The macabre scenes caused Sharon to erupt in the climax of an orgasm. She panted excessively as she caught her breath. A new addiction was now carved into her heart. As beads of sweat formed on her forehead she didn't hesitate to repeat the process many times over until nightfall replaced the day. Her urge to masturbate, while thinking of horrid bloody thoughts replaced her body's need for nourishment at the present time. Her chief macabre thought was the horrific murder of

Touch. She replayed the scene over and over in her mind and used that image as a springboard for reaching an orgasm. Besides providing a safe haven to masturbate, Sharon learned that the basement was the perfect place to eavesdrop on her roommates. She listened intently as their thoughts were broadcast through the ventilation system by way of them talking on the phone, hosting company or by simply talking to each other. She now claimed the basement as her personal dwelling place, so much so that she moved all of the contents of her room into the basement that very day. Sharon also noticed that on this day of change and discovery she heard not a peep from Sheila. Sharon nearly wrote that fact off as Shelia agreeing with her thoughts and actions.

Sheila convinced Sharon to go on a trip and visit her mother at the Norristown State Hospital. Sharon willfully did so, for she was full of spite and mischief. The more she thought of Vera's former self, the more she wanted to destroy what she had become. In Sheila's point of view, Vera wasn't even a shell of her former self, she was but a wraith that only somewhat resembled Vera. Sheila also thought that this new Vera should be "destroyed" so that the memory of what Vera used to be could live on. Surprisingly, Sharon agreed totally.

THE SHARON SLAUGHTER STORY

Sharon arrived at the mental hospital with a mind full of troublesome gambits all aimed at destroying Vera's well-being. Too anxious to wait on an elevator, Sharon walked up a few flights of stairs to get to Vera's room. Once she reached Vera's room and laid eyes on her, she was a bit taken back by her appearance. Vera looked as if she had aged twenty years since Sharon's last visit. Sheila likened Vera's appearance to that of a sick dog that needed to be put out of her misery.

"Momma! Momma! It's me Sharon! Momma don't you remember me?" said Sharon like a sad little puppy.

Vera didn't respond in the slightest bit, she merely stared off into space. A wicked grin crossed Sharon's face as Sheila took control of her thoughts. Reaching into her purse, Sharon pulled out a small piece of paper that looked identical to the small piece of paper that Vera once coveted. Sharon waved the item in Vera's face. Upon seeing the paper, Vera came to life. Again and again she tried in vain to obtain the paper, but try as she might, Sharon would not let her grasp it. The cat and-mouse game became a sight to behold, as Vera rose to her feet and charged Sharon. Quite the agile prankster, Sharon dodged Vera's advance while at the same time sticking her foot out and tripping Vera. Floored, Vera stood up, gathered herself and charged at Sharon once again. Sharon responded by jumping on Vera's bed, thus once again thwarting her aggressive advance. Vera pursued Sharon around the room for several harsh minutes, before Sharon took the chase outside the room. Sharon led Vera past aloof nurses and into the very same staircase she climbed to get to her room. There, she once again reached into her purse but this time she produced a handful of small pieces of paper that were identical to the one Vera once beheld. Sharon waited until Vera was literally close on her heels before she launched the handful of papers down the staircase. Vera responded by diving down the staircase, head first. The sound of her body tumbling down the staircase caused Sharon to shriek in a high-pitched laughter. The only negative aspect to the scene for Sheila and Sharon, was that Vera remained alive.

"I don't know what the fuck she be doing down there but she stay locked in and singing like a dying dog! Maybe she don't feel like part of the team. Roxanne let's knock on the door and try to kick it with her!" exclaimed Rasheeda as she grabbed Roxanne by the shoulder in an honest eff ort to lead her to the basement.

Roxanne shook her head "no" in apparent apprehension. Undeterred, Rasheeda ventured to the basement door and knocked with firmness. Moments later a quiet disheveled looking Sharon answered the door.

"Sharon why don't you go out with us? It will be fun gurl! We could like go downtown to Dances tonight! It will be really fun and the niggas will be there! Come on! I will dress you! Gurl come on," urged Rasheeda as she grabbed Sharon by the arm and whisked her up to her room.

Sharon moved unmethodically as she let Rasheeda take control. Over the course of six hours, Rasheeda reconfigured Sharon from head to toe. Periodically, Roxanne and Paula would stop in Rasheeda's room to catch a glimpse of the amazing transformation. Rasheeda talked through the entire makeover. She told tales of raunchy sex and of her many paramours. Particularly, a rapper named Cool C. For Rasheeda was a ghetto trophy piece, a signifying marker that all young males dreamt to behold. Sharon spoke very little but Sheila was buzzing in her mind with rampant thoughts.

'Rasheeda is pretty I wonder what she tastes like Sharon! Do this bitch ever stop talking? Sharon she acting like your friend! Slit her throat she trying to set you up! Kill her Sharon! Sharon I wonder how the Y-incision would look on her chest? Bite her in the face!'

Sharon somehow managed to ignore Sheila's rants. With the makeover complete, Rasheeda showed Sharon herself in the full-length mirror. Sharon was amazed at her chic appearance. Sheila was also stunned. Sharon's look reminded her of Vera in her prime. The other roommates were equally flabbergasted. Sharon's beauty rivaled Rasheeda's in form and posture. Jealousy was in the air as everyone tried in vain to surpass Sharon's glamour. Heading out to the popular youth nightclub in Paula's vehicle, the women all felt a surge of joyous exuberance. The night was young and they all felt that a good time was on the horizon. They sang tunes together and told off hand jokes to everyone's delight. It was a good moment in Sharon's life. She felt like the group truly accepted her. Sheila on the other hand was suspicious.

'Sharon they ain't taking you to no fucking club gurl! They trying to kill you! Reach in your purse and put a blade in your hand. The first one to make a move, you slit her throat.'

Sharon ignored Sheila's warnings while the group arrived at the nightclub without any malicious events. Once they found an ideal parking spot, Paula turned down the radio and made a speech.

"Pussy make the world go round! Ladies we know the rules but I'm gonna repeat them because this Sharon's first time going out with us to the club. So here go the rules! Number one, we came together so we leave together. We don't go to no nigga house!

They come to ours! Number two, we always working! Keep your eyes wide for niggas with bank that we can set up and take down! And last but not least number three. If we get separated in the club make it your business to get back to the car when the club close! This where we meet at so I'm a leave the doors open."

The women all nodded in agreement as they exited the vehicle. Walking, they decided to stay in two groups. Roxanne would stay with Paula and Rasheeda would pair up with Sharon. Entering the club, Sharon was taken back by the blaring loud music and the sweaty bodies that pressed up against each other in rhythm. The scene itself made her core being shutter with sexual tension. It seemed all the guys in the club knew Rasheeda. Sharon noticed this fact and silently steamed with envy.

'Sharon this bitch Rasheeda done fucked the room!' yelled Sheila in Sharon's head. Sharon tried to ignore Sheila's last rave but Rasheeda's popularity made her agree. Rasheeda led Sharon to a back wall where she spoke in her ear.

"Sharon do you know how to dance?"

Sharon shook her head no as she smiled shyly.

"Do like me continued," continued Rasheeda as she began to perform a dance named the Butterfly.

Sharon tried her best to imitate Rasheeda, but her attempts were of comic proportions. In seconds, males flocked around Rasheeda and Sharon. Before Sharon knew it, she was pushed up against the wall and abraised by jean padded penises. Sharon looked to her left and saw Rasheeda was sandwiched between two males. To her right she saw Roxanne and Paula under the same circumstances. In awkward fashion, Sharon tried to look normal. It was of no use. She was in a very uncomfortable situation, however. Sheila was more than willing to step into the forefront. Sharon eased her mind and let Sheila control her movements, which at first was a simple twist of the hips. Slowly but surely, her movements turned into an all-out assault on the two penises to her front and rear. The high tempo of the drumline in the fast-paced music matched her lucid gyrations. The two male dancers begin to struggle to keep pace with her pelvic thrusts. Many club goers began to take notice of Sharon's display of provocative dance moves. Before long, the majority of the club had surrounded her act. Sharon had stolen the show! She was the night's sensation! The present La Femme Fatale members watched in awe. They could never have imagined that Sharon would have danced the way she did. Little did they know Sharon was just as surprised as they were. Sharon went on dancing throughout the night with multiple partners. Many males tried in vain to secure a number to contact Sharon. It was of no use. All Sharon did was remain silent and dance the night away.

"Sharon shut up! I made the crowd go wild! You're no dancing ass ain't have a clue what to do!"

"I was in the grove Sheila! I can dance!"

"Bitch fuck all of that shit! What about how your little girlfriends is acting? Real fucking friendly! Remember what that tall bitch said!"

"I remember! But I just don't think it's one of them! I mean they are pretty cool."

"Pretty cool? Bitch you sound like a dippy white girl! Wake up and pay attention!

"Sheila! I---."

Sharon's loud argument with her alter ego was interrupted by a loud thump of knocking on her basement room door.

"Sharon who the fuck you talking to down there. What you got company? Gurl come on up to the living room we got a meeting!"

It was Kitty and her voice revealed her anger. Sharon quickly got dressed and found her way to the living room where all the La Femme Fatale members were present. The show, "Living Single" played on the television as Kitty stood in the center of the living room.

"Pussy make the world go round! Y'all ain't think to call a bitch before y'all went out and had a fuckin ball! It's okay cause I was out today handling business," said Kitty as her eyes shot daggers around the room. "Earlier today I went to Mamai Lucia and had her give me a spiritual reading," she continued as serious glances went around the room. "Yeah I know y'all like what the fuck I'm doing right? That's the same shit I said cause I originally went in there to do that bitch! But it's something about her old, oily, sexy, weird ass! I wanted to hear what she had to say right. Check this shit out, the bitch said basically that Chronicle ain't shit. Like he don't believe a bitch can have a crew and stand beside his black ass as ah equal! I swear I thought that shit in the back of my mind and I never told anybody that shit! That bitch creeps me out!"

Sharon sulked in her seat. She knew how that experience felt. Kitty went on and on for what seemed like hours about Chronicle's folly as Sharon tuned out the room to indulge in Sheila's barrage of thoughts in her mind.

'Look at this high yellow bitch Kitty! She just thinks she top shit with her cell phone! Sharon why don't you bite a chunk out of her pregnant ass stomach! Maybe you can chew off one of her baby's legs! Chronicle! Chronicle! Chronicle! All this bitch talk about is Chronicle! Nigga sound like a newspaper! We should go find his ass, sauté and fry

his ass so she can shut the fuck up! Kill her! Kill her! Kill all of them!'

"No Sheila," rumbled Sharon in the middle of Kitty talking. The women all looked at Sharon in confusion.

"I'm sorry I was just thinking about the stories!" said an embarrassed Sharon. After another short spell of Kitty's banter, Sharon just couldn't deny Sheila's requests. The temptation was just too great. Sheila's thirst for blood had to be quenched. Sharon had to act fast before she hurt someone.

"Kitty could you please run me to Tradewinds and then to the horse stable up Parkside?" she blurted out. The room broke out into numerous looks of a mixture of curiosity and confusion. Sharon, feeling the anxiety of being the center of attention, explained her request.

"I have to pick up a few things at Tradewinds, you know the pet store on 40th and Market? Then I need to shoot past the horse stable to see if I can get some horse tranquilizer. What?"

Kitty obliged without question. She simply bid the remaining females farewell and escorted Sharon out the front door to her vehicle. However, once the two were alone and out of the hearing range of the other females, Kitty began to speak again.

"Sharon what's up with you? You okay? I know it's been a lot going on lately and I ain't been able to kick it with you like I should be."

Kitty paused as she changed lanes.

"So I just want you to know that you're my ace-in-the-hole. I mean I knew Paula since I was eight and Rasheeda and Roxanne since I was ten. But they ain't about that dumb shit like you is. I know you're a little bit younger than us but bitch you down by law. The other girls probably be jealous of you and talk shit behind your back! Don't sweat it tho! They probably talk about me! Do they?"

Sharon was flattered at Kitty's attempt to draw her into a deeper realm of friendship. But Sheila induced paranoia would not allow her to feel compassion for Kitty. She had listened in secret to her roommates tell tales of Kitty playing them against each other in numerous ways to test their loyalty. Sheila perceived this as one of those attempts. Sharon would play right into Kitty's hands.

"Yeah they talk about you Kitty! They think you believe in Chronicle more than you believe in us! They be saying you spend too much time worrying about his crew and not worrying about us!" said Sharon in melodramatic fashion.

Kitty turned beet-red as she pounded on the steering wheel in anger. Sheila laughed hysterically in Sharon's mind, for she believed she could control

Kitty with careful manipulative maneuvers of the tongue.

"That's insane! See! See! My own team looking at me funny cause I do so much for this nigga and he don't even give me credit! Nigga don't even think I'm his fuckin' equal! I just can't do it no more! I'm leaving this nigga before I lose my fuckin' team! Fuck that!" roared Kitty as she broke out into a fit of crying.

Sharon patted Kitty on her back to show a bit of support. In the moments that followed, Kitty verbally hatched a plan to leave Chronicle and to move La Femme Fatale into the criminal big leagues. By the time they arrived at Tradewinds, Kitty had regained her composure and focus.

"Sharon what the fuck is you getting from out of here?"

"Rabbits! Rabbits Kitty!"

"Sharon, what the fuck for?"

"I'm gonna scalp them!"

"Scalp? Like a fuckin Indian?"

"Yeah! Just like that!"

When the pair entered the pet store, the stench was too great for Kitty's pregnant senses. She quickly elected to wait for Sharon in the vehicle. The small, packed pet store struck an intimate chord within

Sharon. She took in the sights of the variety of animals on display, all registered in her mind as potential pray for her to slaughter. Jovially breezing through every corner of the store, she finally laid eyes on her intended victim. Only they were not rabbits but two Asians who owned the store. Locking eyes with the unaware owners, her mind flashed back to Charlee's dramatic demise. Her blood pressure rose as her hand found the trusty sharpened stiletto in her purse. In a flash, she cornered the female co-owner in a back corner of the store that was designated for dog food. Sharon pointed to a certain brand that was located in the far corner to divert the woman's attention. As the woman turned her back Sharon poised herself for an assault.

"Sharon! What the fuck are you doing! Why are you taking so long! Ain't no fuckin rabbits back here! Gurl come on!" said Kitty startling Sharon.

She discreetly dropped the stiletto back into her purse as the Asian owner led the way to the feeder section. Kitty complained along the way while Sharon replayed Charlee's grizzly homicide in her mind. Once they reached the feeder section, Sharon's attention was captured by the vast number of white mice, rats and rabbits. She pictured herself scalping them all. Sheila firmly objected.

'Bitch what is you doing! Sharon you know all these chink muthafuckas is related! They all are

Charlie! They killed Charlee! Fuck killing rabbits! Kill Charlie!'

"No Sheila!" blurted out Sharon through clenched teeth. Luckily no one noticed her outburst. She quickly selected the two largest rabbits she could find, paid the agreed-upon price for them and hurried Kitty out the pet store. Kitty said nothing as she quickly found her way to the horse stable in the Parkside section of West Philadelphia. It was agreed that Sharon would obtain what she needed from the horse stable in speed, while Kitty waited in the vehicle. The plan went on without a hitch. However, when Sharon returned to the vehicle, Kitty was in a full-scale argument on her cell phone with none other than Chronicle. Sharon listened intently as Kitty called Chronicle every vile word she could imagine. She could now actually perceive that Kitty was indeed on the verge of leaving Chronicle. Kitty was so engulfed in her argument that she didn't even say goodbye when she dropped Sharon off at the La Femme Fatale hideout. Sharon could care less, she had her rabbits and horse tranquilizer. She couldn't wait to get to work on the poor defenseless animals.

Sharon awoke to the sound of raucous laughter. The voice belonged to Kitty. Sharon looked at her alarm clock and took note of the early hour. She couldn't understand the reason for Kitty's early visit. Eavesdropping on a conversation between Kitty and Paula, she comprehended that Kitty had left Chronicle and moved into the house late on the previous day. Sharon reasoned that the event had to have taken place after the dissection of her two rabbits. The thought caused her eyes to wander across the room to the sight of that wicked mutilation. There, two rabbit scalps adorned her dresser in air sealed mason jars. Another thought crossed her mind that made her jump to her feet and take possession of the two jars and an additional one that also adorned her dresser. Gingerly, she skipped up the basement staircase and made her appearance in the living room where Kitty and Paula currently resided.

"Look ya'll," she said happily as she handed two jars to Kitty and one jar to Paula. Confused, they merely looked at the jars before reality struck Kitty.

"Sharon are these the fuckin' rabbit scalps? Ewww! Get this shit away from me! gasped Kitty as she shoved the two jars into Sharon's bosom.

Alarmed, Paula questioned the item she possessed.

"Sharon what the fuck is this?"

"Touch's dick," replied Sharon with a smile on her face. Paula hurled the jar onto the couch in horror.

Sharon laughed an insidious laugh.

After Sharon collected her gruesome jars, Kitty continued her latest news.

"Like I was saying, yesterday Chronicle and them crazy muthafuckas done killed Mamai Lucia's other son Reno and some other muthafuckas that was with 'em! Smoked them niggas like hickory bacon! I was supposed to do Lucia's ass yesterday too but I told you what happened with that! Anyways, Imma just stay here for a while until Chronicle get his shit together. He's gonna need me! But I'm not gonna do shit for his ass until he beg me on his black ass knees! Fuck that! But in the meantime, I'm gonna watch his sneaky ass and see what he gonna do without me, cause I will be damned if I see another bitch on his arm! I made that nigga! You know what I'm saying? Tonight Paula you and me gonna go up to his house in your car and watch his ass! Fuckin sorry ass nigga! I love him tho damn! I can't believe he didn't believe in me!" A wave of emotion hit Kitty, as tears flowed down her cheeks.

Paula tried in vain to console Kitty but Sharon beat her to the deed. Sharon and Paula locked eyes in a glance of shared dislike they quietly shared for each other at that point. Regaining her composure she continued to speak.

"Since I'm going to be staying here we gonna have to make some changes round here! My due date is in the beginning of November so Imma need a room! But I'm not fuckin with no basement! Hell to the no! I'm gonna holla at Roxanne's big ass so I can get her room. I think she should be in the basement with all her work out shit. Sharon I want you to move back into your room upstairs so I can keep an eye on your crazy ass! I know this only a little ass four-bedroom house but, we gonna have to make it work for now. We gonna do big things later, watch!" Sharon and Paula shook their heads in agreement. Sheila however had a different opinion on the matter.

'Sharon this bitch Kitty is out to kill you! Soon as you close your eyes to sleep she gonna kill you! Kill her now! Gut that bitch and hang her baby with her guts! And Paula with her! Look at her goofy bug-eyed ass! Kill her too! Cut them both up! Kill Sharon! Kill! Kill!'

It took everything Sharon had to quietly resist Sheila's vile demands. But try as she might, she could not shut out Sheila's voice from her mind. She knew some absurd behavior had to be manifested to settle the raging storm that was Sheila.

"Okay Sheila I hear you! For now let's go see Vera!" Sharon mumbled in a tone so low that neither Kitty nor Paula could hear her.

The remark quieted Sheila for the moment and gave Sharon a chance to think of another dastardly way to put Vera out of her misery.

THE SHARON SLAUGHTER STORY

Since the last fiasco at the mental institution, Vera had been moved to a more secure wing that was more equipped to handle a violent outburst. Arriving just past lunchtime, Sharon noticed the upgrade in security. She giggled to herself as she imagined the chaos she would soon cause with Sheila's help. Making it to the entrance of Vera's room, Sharon was greeted by a gruff overweight male who undressed Sharon with his eyes immediately when he saw her. Picking up on the dirty look, Sharon pictured herself slitting the man's throat. This thought caused her to smile in a very coy and sly manner.

"You must be Miss Malo's daughter huh? Wow have a nice visit and let's not have another episode like last visit! Now if you need any help I will be right over there at my station. Ok? By the way my name is Dennis and I'm a Virgo," said the male nursing attendant. Sharon rolled her eyes and glided into Vera's room like a phantom.

She quickly found a chair and moved it closer to Vera who lay motionless on a small twin-size bed. Vera looked at the ceiling in a trance-like state as her bald, patched up hair and single arm cast gave her a sad and miserable appearance. Sharon sat still in silence while her eyes studied Vera. She wished upon a star that the Vera she had come to love so long ago would surface and get herself back to her old ways.

That wish fell on dead hopes. For Vera clearly would never be as she was. This fact alone made Sharon beam with hatred and contempt for Vera. After a tense period of just staring at Vera maliciously, Sharon decided to take action. First, she set her sights on the location of the male nurse attendant. He was busy yakking away on the phone and not paying her even the slightest bit of attention. Feeling the time was ripe, she produced yet another small piece of paper that formerly caused Vera to come to life. It was a perfect, exact replica of the same piece of paper that was given to Vera on the very day Sharon was born. Before she allowed Vera to lay eyes on the tiny piece of paper, she opened a nearby window and peered out of it, judging its height from the ground. She reasoned that the window was at least two stories high. Now she wished that the fall from the window would finally lead to Vera's death. Switching her focus, she dangled the piece of paper in front of Vera. In an instant, Vera came to life. Even though one of her arms was in a cast, she still moved vigorously to grab the small piece of paper. The raging movement landed Vera on the floor. Then she crawled towards Sharon who raced to the window and waited for her to draw closer. When Vera reached Sharon's feet, Sharon helped her stand up while still managing to keep the small piece of paper away from her. Sharon then held the piece of paper out the window and released Vera. Before Vera could get a grasp on the paper Sharon let the paper go into the breezy air. Vera slowly climbed the windows ledge and dived for the airborne, tiny piece of paper. Vera fell into a nearby hedge of bushes. She suffered numerous broken bones and a fractured skull, but her life remained intact to the disappointment of both Sharon and Sheila.

It was 4 AM and Sharon was restless. With the recent addition of Kitty's presence, the house seemed to be in an uproar. The latest gossip brought fuss of Kitty and Paula laying eyes on Chronicle consorting with the enemy. Specifically, the culprit was a tall gangly woman who was known as Mamai Lucia's aide. Silently, Sharon wondered if it was the same tall woman that read her fortune. Kitty regaled the roommates with the story into the wee hours of the morning until they all fell asleep except Sharon. Sleep evaded her as Sheila plagued her mind with thoughts of bloody homicide and conspiracy theories.

'Sharon get up! How are you gonna sleep when everybody in the house is plotting to kill you? They all sleep you can kill them all right now. Get up! Kitty is lying to throw you off her ass! It's the same tall bitch you went and saw! She told Kitty everything! She knows that you know she really is your enemy! If you don't kill her I will! Watch me!'

BLACK MAMBA

Sharon opened her eyes and saw an image of Sheila leaving her room with a certain blade in her hand. Sharon looked into her nightstand and found the exact same blade. Stumbling to her feet she whispered for Sheila to come back. Her words fell on deaf ears. Sheila was already creeping into Kitty's room. Following suit, Sharon also eased into Kitty's room without making a sound. Sheila seemed to have disappeared into thin air leaving Sharon standing alone with a blade in her hand staring at a deeply sleeping Kitty. Sharon slowly made her way over to Kitty until she was in arms reach. She watched as Kitty's chest rose and fell with her breathing. Feelings of insane, bizarre madness invaded Sharon's bloodstream as she raised the blade high in the air. All she could see was herself stabbing Kitty until her arm was tired. She bit her lip in wicked anticipation of the coming blood splatter. Bracing herself for the violet melee, her attack was thwarted by the ringing of Kitty's cell phone. Sharon immediately dropped to the floor and rolled underneath Kitty's bed in surprised fright. She looked to her left and there she saw Sheila putting a finger across her lips gesturing her to be quiet. Sharon obliged without question. The sound of Kitty erupting in anger filled not only the room, but the entire house.

"No fuck you Chronicle! You lying, you ain't get shot! I saw you hugged up with that lanky ass tall bitch that run with Mamai Lucia! You think you slick but I'm not slow! You can keep that pole long bitch!

I'm done with you! No! No! No!" Sharon could hear Kitty move from the bed to the bathroom. She listened so intensely that she could hear Kitty urinate while sobbing. Sharon peered to her right and saw Sheila running to her room. That was her cue to follow suit. In a few quick motions she made it to her feet and into the hallway where she ran into Paula. Feeling like the jig was up, she darted into her room and slammed the door shut. Paula waved off the incident as her catching Sharon and Kitty in a late-night lesbian affair.

Sharon found herself alone and bored late one muggy summer night. Rasheeda was off on a date and the rest of the house was engaged in a raid on Chronicle's house. That left Sharon alone full of mischief and adventure. Going on a minor raid herself, she invaded Rasheeda's room and stole a number of her provocative garments for her plan. Quickly, she got dressed and viewed herself in the mirror before she left. What she saw was the spitting image of Vera in her prime. Satisfied, she galloped out the house and into the heat of the night. Strutting down Main Street, she did her best to walk as seductively as she could. Her eff ort was indeed effective. For many vehicles stopped and almost caused accidents at the sight of her appearance.

Sharon loved the attention and Sheila didn't object. It was a harmony made in hell. Sharon put on this act until she reached a bar called the "Happy Inn" on the edge of the Darby/Philadelphia borderline near Island Avenue. She made her way to the bar out of sheer curiosity. There, she found the bar crowded to capacity and filled with loud blaring music. Sheila wanted nothing more, than to join the dance crowd but Sharon hated the small space. After a brief moment of arguing with Sheila, Sharon briskly left the bar and crossed Island Avenue into Philadelphia.

Activity to her right across Woodland Avenue caught her attention. There she noticed barely dressed women walking back and forth as if they were on display for the passing vehicles on Island Avenue. Inspecting the crowd, Sharon saw that Sheila was amongst the women. Pausing for a brief moment to ponder what the women were actually doing, a beat-up seemingly ancient, pickup truck pulled over close to her as the sound of its horn jolted her out of her thoughts. Sharon cautiously walked over to the pickup truck and glared through its window. The driver was a middle-aged Caucasian man with a long beard. He reminded Sharon of a truck driver.

"I got seventy-five for a half and half," said the dingy looking man as he dangled currency in his hand.

It was then that Sharon realized she was smack-dab in the middle of a prostitution stroll. A slight evil grin formed on her lips as she entered the pickup truck and took the currency without uttering a word. The man smiled before he made a sharp U-turn and then a sharp right onto a small street next to Paschal housing projects. One final right turn on another small street named Lloyd and then the man decided to park. The street was desolate and dark. Sharon could tell from the man's comfort level that he had done this routine many of times. He leaned his seat-back unzipped his pants and exposed his small penis. Sharon smiled a sly grin while she eased her face closer to the man's penis. Inches away, Sharon hesitated to touch the man's penis due to the foul stench of sweat that emanated from his groin. Before she could react, the man used his hands to force her head upon his penis. Surprised, Sharon latched onto his scrotum sack with her teeth. She clamped on with all the strength she could muster. Yelling in pain the man tried in vain to beat her off. In the midst of the struggle Sharon ripped off one of the man's testicles. The man quickly exited the pickup truck and tried to seek help. He did so with his pants around his ankles and legs covered in blood. Exiting the pickup truck, Sharon put the currency in her purse and spit out the lone testicle onto the sidewalk. Almost effortlessly, she sashayed back to Island Avenue and joined the ranks of the lively group of prostitutes. There she encountered strange looks and aggressive word play.

"Oh no little bitch you can't work this stroll!"

"Who you looking for?"

"Bitch you better work that gas station side!"

"You better get your ass up!"

Sharon smiled as she produced a rather large blade from her purse. Upon seeing the blade, the prostitutes promptly crossed the street and did not say another word. Alone, Sharon knew not what she should be doing. Looking across Island Avenue she took note of the prostitutes' actions and mimicked them perfectly. She did so well that a slew of vehicles honked their horns in an effort to get her attention. The attention was what Sharon and Sheila both craved like a narcotic. Sharon was so caught up in the moment that she didn't even notice a pair of patrol cars park to her right on Woodland Avenue. The two patrol cars held four police officers who exited their vehicles and split into two groups. They began to walk on both sides of Island Avenue towards Sharon. The group that occupied across Island Avenue from Sharon began to question the group of prostitutes. While the other group that was on Sharon's side closed in on her without her immediate knowledge. By the time she noticed them it was too late. They had her surrounded and began to question her about a man that had one of his testicles bitten off. Sharon evaded their questions in a very coy manner. Suddenly, a vehicle whizzed past Sharon and the police officers, yelling obscenities in a familiar tone.

"Bitch what the fuck is you doing out here? Selling pussy?

Get your ass over to the gas station and get the fuck in the car!"

It was Kitty along with Paula and Roxanne was driving. Sharon promptly excused herself from the presence of the police officers and made her way across Island Avenue to the gas station. Entering the rear passenger seat, she quickly closed the vehicle's rear door and made a request.

"Please Roxanne can you go back around that little block over there? The one with the little like playground at the end! I left something! Please!" Roxanne obliged without question.

Once the group arrived on Lloyd Street they found a small police presence. Paranoid, Roxanne commanded Sharon to find her lost item with speed. Sharon successfully did so without alerting the police that patrolled the small street. She noticed that the Caucasian man's pickup truck was still parked in the same spot. Away from obvious trouble back in Darby, a curious Kitty questioned Sharon about the mysterious item she just had to have.

"A white man's nut I bit off!" Sharon answered casually as the entire group stared at her in bewilderment.

"We out hitting Chronicle for all his work and shit right? And here this crazy ass bitch is chewing on cracka nuts! Unfucking believable!" yelled Kitty as the group joined her in laughter.

After Sharon's latest episode, the group made a decision not to leave her unattended ever again, if possible. To make this happen, they chose to take turns babysitting her. Drawing straws, it was determined that Paula was up first. For Paula, this was the worst possible scenario, being that she was also in charge of distributing the cache of stolen narcotics the group had recently commandeered from Chronicle. Paula was livid to say the least. Her face showed every bit of emotion.

"Rules are rules o girl! So you gotta take her with you when you go do what you got to do! The rest of us gonna be right here till you get back!" said Rasheeda laughing as the rest of the La Femme Fatale members agreed with her logic.

Sharon sat bright eyed with a grin on her face. She couldn't wait to see what activities awaited her while in Paula's company.

"Oh my fuckin God! Whatever!"

"Sharon go get your purse or whatever you got right now because I got shit to do! And bitch you better not bite nobody! Come on!" ordered Paula in frustration.

Sharon literally ran out the living room up to her room and returned in the blink of an eye. She followed closely as Paula stormed out of the house. Once the pair got settled in Paula's vehicle, Paula had more choice words for Sharon.

"Just sit back in the seat and chill ok? Don't do no nut shit! Now we gotta go around Colorado Street where you bit that boy Van dick off! I don't want him to see you 'cause I don't know what he might do. They say Tim ain't been around since Sandra and Rachel's old boyfriends robbed them. So I guess we cool. Oh shit, I forgot! I sideswiped that damn block!

Fuck maybe it ain't safe to go round there just yet! What you think Sharon?"

Sharon tilted her head to the side as if she was pondering the situation before she spoke.

"If we go and something go wrong, I can bite our way out! That's a whole lot of dicks I could be collecting!"

Paula shook her head in fright as a nervous laugh escaped her mouth. Here she was hell-bent on trafficking narcotics and in the meantime she had to babysit a pit-bull in a skirt. She decided to not divulge any more of her plans to Sharon. In her mind it was of no use because she believed Sharon was indeed insane.

The pair arrived near Colorado Street after a forty-five minute drive. In the spirit of caution, Paula opted to park on nearby 17th Street.

"Ok now here is the plan: I'm gonna walk around the corner and see if these niggas is tryna grab this work here," said Paula as she reached across Sharon's lap and retrieved a plastic shopping bag from the glove compartment.

Before Sharon could form her lips to ask a question, Paula gave a detailed answer.

"It's crack! Three ounces bagged up into swirls! Gurl a swirl is a quarter of an ounce. It's four swirls in an ounce. So we got twelve swirls to get rid of, at ah hundred and fifty. So how much we gonna make?

"Eighteen hundred!" Sharon blurted out immediately.

Paula nodded her head in approval. Apparently, Sharon did display a certain level of intelligence in between her fits of insanity.

Paula continued, "So like I was saying I'm gonna walk round this corner and see if these niggas wanna buy this work. When they hear the price they gonna be going crazy! Plus, this Chronicle shit, so I know it's fire! But check this out right. I ain't been down here since you bit ol' boy and I sideswiped damn near the whole block. So I don't know how they going to act. To be safe I'm only gonna take like three of these jawns. But if you see me running back to the car, get behind the wheel and get ready to drive the fuck outta here! You can drive right?"

Sharon blinked absentmindedly before answering.

"Yeah girl of course!"

"Ok then Imma leave the car running. I will be right back!" said Paula in excitement.

In her mind she truly felt she was on the verge of making a social connection with Sharon. Exiting the vehicle, she made sure she secured the narcotics in her bra before she walked to Colorado Street. Sharon watched as Paula turned the corner and disappeared out of sight. Seconds later, Sharon broke out into a bitter argument with Sheila out loud.

"Sharon why are you just sitting here like a fuckin duck! You know she is going to get that boy I bit to kill you! Take the rest of the crack and run!"

"No Sheila! I can't leave Paula! We have a plan! She is a part of La Femme Fatale!"

"La Femme Fatale? Sharon you stupid bitch! You are La Femme Fatale!"

"Stop it Sheila, not now!"

"Bitch when? Look! Here the bitch Paula go right here running now! What you gonna do drive? You never drove in your fuckin life!"

Sharon jumped over to the driver's seat, put the vehicle in reverse and pressed on the gas pedal as hard as she could, which caused it to slam into the vehicle behind it. As Sharon fumbled with the gear shift Paula managed to climb into the passenger window.

"Put this muthafucka in drive bitch! Get us the fuck outta here!" yelled Paula in fear as a mob of young men ascended on the scene. A brick suddenly broke through the front windshield causing glass to litter the inside of the vehicle. Seizing the moment Paula reached out and grabbed the gear shift, as she put the car in drive Sharon pressed the gas pedal. The car veered wildly into the street narrowly missing a head-on collision with a trash truck. Focusing her sights on the mob, Sharon kept her foot on the gas pedal and turned the steering wheel in their direction. Before she knew it, she had mowed down several mob participants with two remaining on the vehicle's hood, as she crashed into a fi re hydrant. With water spewing into the air and chaos filling the land, Paula quickly moved to Sharon's lap and gained control of the car. She managed to successfully make an escape without further injury.

THE SHARON SLAUGHTER STORY

"No fuck all of that! Bitch I had to haul ass outta there! Them niggas was deep and just my fuckin' luck Tim punk ass was there! He was the main one trying to get me! Oh and Sharon's non-driving ass!" yelled Paula in dramatic comic fashion.

The living room full of La Femme Fatale core members erupted in laughter. None laughed harder than the amused Sharon. Her extreme laughter caused everyone else to stop laughing and stare at her. Kitty silenced the odd moment by speaking in a serious tone.

"Yeah on some real shit, I think we need to dust Tim ass just because! You don't come at no La Femme Fatale members and live to talk about it! I would say draw straws, but this look like a job for Roxanne and that shotgun she got. Roxanne take Sharon with you tonight and wax Tim punk ass!"

Roxanne offered no resistance or formal discrepancy about her task. She merely nodded her head in acceptance as she shared a cynical stare with Sharon. Paula noticed the look and laughed to herself. It was barely noon, which meant the grim deed was hours away from being completed. Kitty and Roxanne chose to use the time to formulate the surefire plan to ensure the deed was done in a way that would prevent Roxanne from being harmed or captured by the authorities. While they planned and plotted Sharon retreated to her room for a similar conversation with Sheila. As soon as she closed her door, she was bombarded with wordplay from Sheila.

"Sharon are you stupid? Roxanne's big ass is gonna shoot you with that muthafukin shotgun! You dumb bitch!"

Eager to respond, Sharon turned up her radio so that no one could hear her conversation.

"Sheila I'm so sick of your evil ass! La Femme Fatale is my only family! They wouldn't hurt me!"

A dark wicked laughter issued from Sharon's mouth. The laughter was so twisted it caused her to look in the mirror. She saw herself, yet she also saw Sheila. Confused, she pulled at her face in an effort to separate herself from Sheila.

"Sharon you stupid dizzy bitch! I am you! You are me!

You can't get rid of me!"

"Sheila shut up! Get away from me! Leave me alone!"

Sharon clawed at her face as she threw her body against her vanity dresser and broke the mirror. Rolling around on the floor she managed to destroy her room. It looked as if a hurricane had blown through it. After a spell of strenuous physical and verbal war with Sheila, Sharon fell to the floor in exhaustion. It was in that state that Kitty found her, hours later.

"Oh my fuckin' God! Sharon! Get your retarded ass up! What the fuck was you in here doing? And why the fuck is your face scratched all the fuck up? Nah! Nah! You ain't going nowhere looking like that! Bitch what was you doing in here?" yelled an appalled Kitty in dismay.

The rest of the house joined Kitty to view the chaotic scene. Sharon rose to her feet wearing the look of a damaged school girl. Her eyes projected innocence but her face showed malice and discord.

"I was dancing! I was just dancing!" yelled Sharon as she turned down the volume on her radio. The household remained speechless. Taking in the sights, no one knew what to make of the situation. The odd silence was broken by a suggestion from Rasheeda.

"Kitty why don't you, Paula and Roxanne go and handle that business while me and Sharon clean up her room and cook dinner. We will be okay trust me."

Kitty shook her head in agreement and led Roxanne and Paula down the stairs. Reaching the bottom step, Kitty turned around and locked eyes with Sharon.

"Rasheeda call my cell phone if anything go wrong! Sharon you better act like you got some muthafukin' sense!" barked Kitty meaning every word she uttered. Sharon smiled before sucking her teeth. Once Kitty and company left the house Rasheeda began to question Sharon.

"Sharon what is wrong with you? I peeked in here and saw you having a fit! Who the fuck is Sheila?"

Sharon's eyes grew large as saucers at Rasheeda's admission. She was shocked and embarrassed beyond belief. Sheila had been her secret for several years. She had to think fast to keep it that way.

"I was just saying Shelia E to myself that's all! Sheila E is my favorite person next to Sade. I just got a little carried away dancing, Rasheeda," she said in hopes of convincing her. Outwardly Rasheeda seemed to accept Sharon's explanation, yet inwardly she thought Sharon was a lunatic. However, something about Sharon's childish demeanor struck a chord with Rasheeda that made her want to guide Sharon in the right direction. From Sharon and Sheila's point of view, they had no idea if Rasheeda was friend or foe. It was with this mindset and while cleaning her room with Rasheeda that Sheila attacked Sharon's brain waves with seeds of hate.

'Sharon! Bitch are you stupid! They left you alone with this Bitch to kill you! You so busy tryna get rid of me you gonna let this hoe bitch sneak you! She said my name! Kill her!'

Sharon did her best to resist Shiela's urges but it was only a matter of time before she had to act on them. Matters became worse when Sharon saw Sheila reach into her nightstand, retrieve a sharpened blade and slit Rasheeda's throat. The image proved to be too much for Sharon to resist. She made her way to the nightstand without raising suspicion and secured a finely sharpened blade exactly like the one she pictured Sheila with. Making her way behind Rasheeda as she cleaned, fate manifested as the doorbell rang and a stern knock at the door could be heard. From the tone of the knock Rasheeda assumed correctly that it was the authorities. Rasheeda quickly made her way to the door and asked who it was without opening it.

"Darby Police Department!" responded an eager police officer as dread filled Rasheeda's heart. She had no clue why the authorities wished to enter their home. Hearing what was transpiring, Sharon also made a correct assumption. She knew that the authorities were there for her. Without hesitation, she dropped the blade and made her way out a window in the kitchen in the blink of an eye. Unfortunately for her, the authorities had the house surrounded and captured her immediately.

In police custody, Sharon learned that her father had reported her as a runaway. She also learned that her whereabouts were, once again, revealed by an unknown source. Unbeknownst to Sharon, Paula was once again that unknown source. After spending some time in custody, it was determined that Sharon's father Lonnie had recommended that she be jailed until she was of legal age because he could not control her. Accordingly, a judge reprimanded her to Sleighton Farms, where she could be confined and still receive an education until she was a legal adult. For Sharon it was a bittersweet moment. She would get the chance to embark on a new adventure, but she would be confined while doing so.

Arriving at Sleighton Farms, Sharon was delighted at the spacious surroundings. It reminded her of an Indian village. Breezing through the tedious intake process, she found herself in a cottage with several female strangers around her age. Immediately, she was questioned by the strangers about her age and what crime landed her in Sleighton. Sharon didn't say a word, she only found her sleeping arrangements and took to a peaceful slumber.

Awakening earlier than the rest of her cottage mates, she saw an image of Sheila leaving the cottage.

Curious, she followed Sheila's lead until she found herself behind The King of Prussia Mall. It was then that reality dawned on her. She had escaped Sleighton Farms! Paranoia set in as she contemplated returning to the farm. As usual, Sheila wasted no time in making a suggestion.

'Sharon if you take your ass back to that kiddy jail camp you will be the absolute dumbest bitch in America! You silly muthafucka, hitch a ride back to Philly.'

After considering several possibilities through her thought process, Sharon took Sheila's advice and successfully hitched a ride back to Philadelphia. Specifically, Love Park in Center City. There, she was on the receiving end of dubious stares from the homeless community. She attributed the malicious looks to her assumed role in the brutal death of Touch. Her only option was to make the long trek to the La Femme Fatale lair in Darby, PA. The walk- on a hot summer day- took three and a half long, hard hours. She argued with Sheila the entire journey. Tired and weary, she knocked on the door and was greeted by a shocked Paula.

"Damn! Bitch you look like you escaped slavery! How did you make it here? That's crazy cause Kitty and Roxanne just left to go rough up your dad so he could get you out of out of that place!" said Paula wearing a facade of concern. Secretly, she wished for Sharon to be locked away for the remainder of her life. Sharon made her way through the front door and fell onto the living room couch in exhaustion. She awoke hours later to the sound of laughter and the smell of pizza. Starving, she followed the aroma to the kitchen where she not only found the pizza, but Kitty, Roxanne, Paula and Rasheeda drinking Taylor Port and smoking marijuana. Kitty, the only sober member of the group of four because of her pregnancy, acknowledged Sharon first.

"Damn Sharon you look tore the fuck up! Here come eat some of this pizza with me before these high ass drunk bitches eat it all up! You need to eat then go wash your ass girl! Oh and don't worry about going back to that farm shit! Me and Roxanne went and hollered at your dad! Tomorrow we gonna go to a lawyer office and start the process to get you out of that farm shit and be a legal adult. Your dad gonna take care of it! I don't think he want Roxanne to put her shotgun up his ass!" roared Kitty as the kitchen boomed in unified laughter.

Sharon felt relieved and elated at the same time. She felt even better when she gorged herself on the hot pizza.

With days passing of recuperation and concentrated eff orts that finally put her legal troubles behind her Sharon sat silently and listened to the latest La Femme Fatale news. As usual Kitty with the voice of central control.

"Pussy make the world go round! Ok y'all we back to business! Sharon done took care of her legal shit and got her father to sign the emancipation papers. She is a legal adult now! No more cops coming to the spot looking for her! Don't know how they knew she was here but that shit over now! Last week Roxanne took care of Tim punk ass! He ain't dead but he got wheels for legs and everybody around Colorado Street know we mean business. Paula done moved all the shit we stole from Chronicle, on her new block Dakota Street. Rasheeda got three new muthafuckas we can jux. A nigga named M-Dot from Parkside that's clocking crazy paper on the weed tip. A nigga named T-Rex from Logan that got all the pancakes and syrup. And a Latin King Puerto Rican muthafucka from Camden, named King Killa. It's gonna take her a while to work this King Killa muthafucka, he's large forreal! But the other two is ready right now! M-Dot locked up, so we gonna break into his crib tonight! We gonna get T-Rex in a couple days so we on point! As for me, my crazy ass baby father done shot his little brother connect Bingo weeks ago but the fat muthafucka aint die! I know what club he hang in so as soon as we take care of business with those other niggas we on him ourselves! That fat muthafucka ain't gonna know what hit him! So is there any questions?"

Sharon raised her hand and Kitty nodded for her to speak.

"I'm hungry. Why can't we go get the pancakes and syrup right now? I mean ain't that breakfast food?" The living room erupted in laughter.

M-Dot was a popular West Philadelphia marijuana distributor. He met Rasheeda while she shopped at 52nd and Market Streets, which was his primary narcotic haven. He was smitten by Rasheeda's beauty and from the first interaction with her he fell head over heels in love. Within the first week of just dating Rasheeda he made the fatal mistake of not only showing her where he lived but also giving her a key. It was then that Paula hatched the plan to call the authorities at an opportune time to get him arrested. The plan worked and the plot thickened with the late-night arrival of Paula, Roxanne, Sharon and Rasheeda at M-Dot's abode. With the key in hand, Rasheeda led the raid as the women ransacked the structure to make it appear as if someone was searching for something. This act was done to make M-Dot believe that someone was looking for his hidden cache of marijuana to take Rasheeda off the suspect list. For she knew exactly where the profitable stash was hidden. M-Dot foolishly showed her the stash to gain bragging rights while trying to impress her.

"It's in the basement hidden in the floor! The floor has a hidden space under the couch down there! Move the couch!" yelled Rasheeda as Roxanne and Sharon followed her instructions.

Finding the marijuana trove, Sharon wasn't thrilled. As the women marveled at the findings, Sharon wandered off into the house. Alone in the upper portion of the house, she found an additional hidden cache that contained currency. The innocent part of Sharon wanted to alert the group to her findings, however, Sheila burst forth in Sharon's mind to quiet that notion.

'Sharon! Bitch are you nuts! That looks like stacks of hundred-dollar bills! It's just enough to tuck in your waist and in your purse! Bitch hide that shit! Here come somebody!'

Sharon moved with speed and granted Sheila her request just before Rasheeda entered the main bedroom behind her.

"Sharon did you find anything in here? That nigga aint show me nothing but weed! I don't know where he hid his money! Gurl we gotta get out of here before somebody spot us let's get this weed and be out!"

Loaded with currency, Sharon exited the house with her secret intact.

Later on, back at the La Femme Fatale hideout, the group relished their latest caper which netted them thirty-four pounds of high-grade marijuana. Sharon, however, locked in her room alone, counted the proceeds from her private take. The grand total was twelve thousand four hundred dollars. She hid the currency in between her mattress and box spring. Laying on her bed buried in her own thoughts, she liked the idea of being a self-centered snake. It seemed to place her in a position to gain power and privilege. Sharon wanted to know what Sheila thought.

"Sheila, being sheisty ain't so bad is it?"

"No jackass! I told you Sharon fuck these lame bitches! We got the power! Look how much money we got doing us! Just do what I say!"

"But Sheila all you wanna do is kill them all! They haven't tried to kill me yet! You're wrong about that!"

"I'm not ever wrong! If they don't try to kill you they gonna try and put you in jail! One of them called the cops on you!" Sharon remained silent.

She was trapped in the thought. She believed Sheila had a point but she didn't have a clue as to who would have done such a thing. Running the possibilities through her mind, Sheila gave her a suspect.

"It's Paula, Sharon! It has got to be that scary bitch! I told you to slit her throat!"

"But Sheila how do you know?"

"Think about it Sharon! Only her and Kitty have cell phones right?"

"Right"

"You was with Rasheeda so she couldn't have done it right?"

"Right"

"And why would Kitty and Roxanne go and scare your father to get you free? Just wait 'til the bitch go to sleep and slit her muthafuckin throat!"

"Ok Sheila!"

Sharon armed herself with a number of blades and concealed them in a small book bag. Looking like a quasi-school student, Sharon left the confines of her room and joined the group's festivities. Marijuana smoke clouded the air as speakers thumped reggae music. Sharon let her vision take in the sights. Immediately she noticed the entire group except Kitty was occupied with packing marijuana. Stepping into the scene Sharon found a seat next to Roxanne who seemed to be weighing marijuana on a midsize scale.

Completely out of her league, Sharon sat back and watched each member and their specific role. Paula made smaller bags of marijuana that Sharon recognized to be ten-dollar bags. Rasheeda also seemed to be making ten-dollar bags but, upon closer inspection, Sharon noticed that Rasheeda's bags were half the size of Paula's. Sharon reasoned that they were five-dollar bags. Leaning in to ask Roxanne what the value of her bags were, Sharon was passed a marijuana cigarette by Rasheeda. Wanting to be a part of the click, Sharon took the marijuana and inhaled its fumes with all her might. Immediately she broke out into a fit of coughing. Everyone in the room laughed. Hearing the laughter, Kitty entered the living room from the kitchen and was caught off guard by Sharon's marijuana mishap. Turning down the loud music, Kitty checked to make sure Sharon was in good health.

"Girl what the fuck is you doing smoking reefer? That shit we took from M-Dot stronger than a muthafucka! Pass that shit on and drink some water," said Kitty with a motherly concern.

The women continued to laugh, making Sharon feel alienated. Relocating to the kitchen to get a glass of water, the euphoric effects of the marijuana took over her being. She perceived that her heart was beating abnormally loud and the spirit of paranoia manifested as additional voices in her mind. Trying her best to overcome the high, Sharon turned to Sheila for help.

"Sheila what the fuck is going on!"

"They laced the joint with something Sharon! They tryna kill you! Kill them first!

"I can't I left my book bag with them I think and everything look funny in the dark! Help me Sheila!"

"Sharon who the fuck is you talkin' to in here in the dark! And why the fuck you got that bookbag on for?" demanded Kitty as she turned on the kitchen light and observed Sharon closely.

Terrified and shocked that she didn't realize she still wore her bookbag, Sharon made a dramatic plea to Kitty.

"Paula called the cops and told them I was here when I was on the run! Imma slit her fuckin throat! And they laced the joint I just smoked! I'm high out of my mind! Imma kill Paula!"

Hearing her name mentioned in true accusation, Paula resembled a deer trapped in headlight as Sharon came charging at her with an acutely sharpened blade. Dashing to Paula's aide, Roxanne knocked Sharon to the ground with a blindsided savage blow to the temple. Floored, Sharon dropped the blade in agony as Roxanne sat on her chest to keep her from regaining her footing. Trapped, Sharing yelled out every horrid, vile, blasphemous, profane word she could think of. Her raging lunatic demeanor sent chills down the spines of everyone present.

"What? I ain't no snitch! Ain't nobody lace no damn joint! See what I mean Kitty? See? You see? This little bitch is crazy! You need to kick this retarded muthafucka to the curb! She ain't no fuckin La Femme Fatale," argued Paula in defense. Outwardly, she appeared to be stern in her denial but inwardly she was a mess. She wondered how Sharon could possibly know that she was indeed the hidden source that tipped off the authorities about Sharon's whereabouts. Kitty stood in between the center of the action. Shaking her head to the tune of her silent thought she too believed that Paula was the anonymous caller. Keeping that belief hidden, she had a perfect solution to the tension between Paula and Sharon. "Ok Paula and Sharon shut the fuck up with that shit! Enough! I'm sick of y'all with that bull shit! Ain't no bad blood between no La Femme Fatale members! So you know what? We gonna move all the furniture in this muthafucka and y'all two bitches gonna rumble! After that, y'all gonna shake hands and this shit gonna be over!"

Sharon, still pinned to the ground by Roxanne, laughed in bizarre fashion. She loved the idea. Paula on the other hand shuttered at the thought of violence, though her words indicated otherwise.

"Rumble? Please! I would mop the floor with that little runt bitch! I'm not beating nobody's fuckin kid! Fuck her!" said Paula in an effort to avoid violence.

Sharon vociferously taunted Paula with extreme vigor. In the midst of the shouting, Kitty and Rasheeda moved the furniture aside and made a makeshift ring in the living room. Kitty made a brief exit from the excitement and returned with a jar of petroleum jelly. She greased Sharon and Paula's faces with the substance. She could feel the fear in Paula and the strife in Sharon. Methodically, she relieved Sharon of her book bag while Roxanne still pinned her to the ground. Finally she gave Paula some words of advice.

"You better fight or get your ass whipped! Roxanne, let Sharon go!"

Roxanne did as she was told and released Sharon. The velocity in which Sharon rose to her feet and chased Paula was almost superhuman. She steamed headfirst into Paula like a bull with horns. The collision sent both females crashing to the floor with Sharon landing on top of Paula.

"No fuckin' biting Sharon! If you bite her Imma let Roxanne knock the shit out of you again," roared Kitty. Sharon threw a barrage of punches in windmill form that all landed in or around the vicinity of Paula's head. This caused Paula to cover her face and fold into a fetal position. Black and blue clouded her vision and a vertigo like dizziness began to cloud her wits. Sharon hammered away while yelling like an Indian warrior.

"That's enough Kitty damn! It's over! Paula ain't fighting back!" pleaded Rasheeda. Kitty gave Roxanne the nod and Roxanne ripped Sharon off of Paula in one swoop and held on to her. Paula struggled to stand up on her feet, when she did, she secured a crystal ashtray and successfully hurled it in Sharon's direction. The projectile grazed Sharon on the left side of her head. The blow only enraged Sharon, who broke free from Roxanne's firm grip and crashed back into Paula. In this round, fighting with her back against the ground, Paula fought back with a sincere sense of urgency. It was of no use. She was no match for Sharon's wild style of hand-to-hand combat. Sharon wanted to hurt Paula so bad she could taste Paula's blood and sweat in her mouth. Her gruesome fantasy was rudely interrupted by a vicious clothesline from Roxanne. Startled and floored, Sharon took a brief moment to rest and refocus her fury. Before she could rise and strike again, Kitty stepped in the middle of the makeshift ring and made an announcement.

"Ok is that the fuck it? Ain't no bad blood in La Femme Fatale! So whoever got beef better speak now or forever hold your peace!" The living room stayed silent for a brief moment until a petroleum greased face Rasheeda's stepped forward.

"I'm sick of Sharon stealing my muthafuckin clothes! I wanna scrap! Fuck that!" Rasheeda rammed a stunned Sharon into a nearby wall with so much force that a large portion of the wall caved in. A wild animal fight ensued in which determining a victor was too daunting of a task. The combatants fought with intense fervor and there seemed to be no end in sight. As the fight raged on, the two females seemed to fight even harder. Locked in pain from gripping each other's hair, Roxanne took the stalemate stance as an opportunity to break up the fight. Kitty then made Rasheeda and Sharon shake hands and hug. When the very same act was ordered for Sharon and Paula, Sharon faked a handshake and hit Paula with a haymaker before embracing her.

Sharon awoke the very next morning sore and scratched up with Vera on her mind. Not wanting to steal an outfit from Rasheeda for fear of reprisal, Sharon opted to wear her own garments. Using some of her secret hidden currency, she caught a cab to the mental institution that housed Vera. Looking at the surrounding hedges, she laughed at the thought of Vera soaring through the air and landing in them.

Making it past a series of nursing attendant checkpoints, she successfully found Vera's room. Sharon noticed that this new room Vera resided in was well fortified and protected. Several nurse attendants remained present in the room for Sharon's visit. Surveying the situation, Sharon was shocked that Sheila had yet to chime into her thoughts. Taking a close look at Vera, Sharon held back laughter. To her, Vera was a pitiful sight to behold. She wished nothing more than to eradicate this form into which Vera had transformed. Wearing a semi body cast, the only thing Vera could move without experiencing pain was her eyes which were glued to the ceiling. Sharon waltzed next to Vera's bed and found a seat. Sharon leaned closer to Vera and whispered into her ear.

"Seven…two…four…five…one…two…four, Sharon!" Immediately Vera began to come to life. She moaned and tried to get up out of her bed. The present nurse attendants flocked to calm Vera down. Once they achieved their goal, they calmly asked Sharon to leave. Defeated, Sharon turned her back on Vera and headed for the room's entrance. Nearly out of the room, Vera's voice struck Sharon's eardrum.

"Sharon! Bitch I know you ain't gonna leave me in this muthafucka you little fat ass heifer!"

THE SHARON SLAUGHTER STORY

T-Rex was another grand narcotics trafficker that made the fatal mistake of being dazzled by Rasheeda. He lived on Camac Street in Logan, but his place of business was in North Philadelphia on 17th and Master Street. His narcotic empire centered around the retail sale of prescription pills (pancakes), Codeine and Promethazine (syrup). He met Rasheeda at Dances nightclub. Under the dim lights and party going atmosphere he was smitten by her Goddess-like beauty. Little did he know his reputation had made him a La Femme Fatale target and his initial meeting with Rasheeda was not by chance. Not even a week after staying in contact with Rasheeda T-Rex began revealing intricate details about his narcotics ring. Another flaw T-Rex displayed was his braggadocio demeanor. Not a second passed in a conversation with Rasheeda without T-Rex boasting about his narcotic proceeds. Rasheeda promptly relayed everything he disclosed to La Femme Fatale. He revealed so much that the speed of his downfall was faster than what it would have been even with La Femme Fatale's greatest efforts.

So it was on this hot midsummer night fate came knocking on his door in the shape of Rasheeda. She had been to T-Rex's house on numerous occasions. She had even spent the night several times. But one thing she did not do was have sex with T-Rex. Holding out on that act drove him insane. So, tonight was special for T-Rex. Rasheeda had promised to have sex with him. Her presence meant his dream was coming true or so he thought. Answering the door fully nude, T-Rex was hit with the butt end of a shotgun. The blow not only caught him totally off guard but knocked him completely off his feet. Bleeding profusely from his left temple, T-Rex stared up at a menacing Roxanne wielding a shot gun.

"Blink and I will be the last bitch you see, nigga" gnarled Roxanne standing over T-Rex.

Whimpering, T-Rex's heart hit the floor when Rasheeda stepped over him and took a seat on his couch. She was joined by Kitty and a happy Sharon. Roxanne kicked the front door shut with a back kick without taking her aim off T-Rex.

"Stop crying like a bitch nigga! We gonna keep this shit short and sweet! We here for the drugs and money! We already know where it's at! Now come sit here next to my homegirl Sharon while me and Rasheeda get all the shit! Move and she will bite your little dick off! Ain't that right Sharon?" said a confident Kitty.

Sharon smiled in delight as she grabbed T-Rex by his arm and sat him down on the couch next to her. There she stared him in the eyes and stroked his penis. There was something in her eyes that scared him deeply. Kitty and Rasheeda took off to different parts of the house. Moments later they returned carrying a host of large bags. Kitty in particular held a small glass jar filled with what looked like Promethazine. Giggling slightly, she ordered T-Rex to drink the concoction. Afraid, held at gunpoint and under Sharon's insane grip, he did so. The group chit-chatted and waited until T-Rex fell into a drug induced slumber before leaving the scene. The next day T-Rex was found dead from a cocktail of prescription drugs. La Femme Fatale had struck again. Their total take was forty-two thousand in currency and a number of large grab bags that contained various prescription narcotics, all valued at around sixty thousand dollars.

Sharon stood silent gazing into the mirror inside her locked bedroom. Through the reflection, she stared at her portion of the proceeds from the last La Femme Fatale caper. Eight thousand dollars. This brought her savings to approximately twenty thousand dollars. She had never possessed that staggering amount in her life. Thinking deeply, she owed it all to being a vicious opportunist and agreeing with Sheila.

"Sheila," said Sharon lightly out loud.

"What bitch! No don't call me now! I told you we run the world!"

"You right Sheila! Fuck everybody else! All we need is each other!"

"Yes bitch I told you! We run La Femme Fatale! Kitty just do the talking! Fuck all them bitches! Let's go downstairs and get another round with Rasheeda! This time put a razor blade under your tongue and slice the bitch!"

"Yeah! Yeah! You right Sheila! Fuck that! Lets—."

"Sharon! Come downstairs and kick it with us! We got a meeting!"

Kitty shouted while banging on Sharon's room door and interrupting her conversation with Sheila. Sharon quickly located a razor blade and placed it under her tongue before leaving her room to join the group in the living room. With all the women settled, Kitty took the floor.

"Pussy make the world go round! Ok ladies we did good yesterday at T-Rex spot! But we can do better! Straight up my soon-to-be baby father doing big things! We can ---."

"Kitty why you always talking about your baby dad? We got it goin' on! We better than them niggas! Check us out!" boasted Sharon cutting Kitty off. Sharon was indeed being influenced by Sheila. Kitty grimaced before laughing slightly. She felt Sharon was trying to challenge her authority.

"Yeah, you right gurl but listen to what I'm saying before you start running off at the mouth! My baby dad doing big things and I know all his plans and we can do what he trying to do before he do it. And we can do that shit better! Now all that pancake and syrup shit we got from T-Rex punk ass gonna go to Paula. She gonna move that shit through them niggas on Dakota Street. That's why she wasn't there on the jux tip cause her job is to move the shit. You feel me? While she moving the shit, Rasheeda can focus on the King Killa shit. But while all this shit is going on we gonna all play the club till we spot this fat nigga named Bingo. He the next big target! My baby daddy was 'pose to smoke his ass but he only shot em. We gonna do his ass in and rob him! Matter of fact, when we got his fat ass where we want him, Sharon since you got all that fuckin lip you gonna eighty-six his ass! You hear me? You got a problem with that?" hissed Kitty staring Sharon in the eyes.

Sharon laughed sadistically and replied with glee.

"I aint got no muthafuckin problem with that! Shit Imma scalp that nigga! Watch!"

The End